A Dark
RAINBOW
RHYTHM & ROMANCE

ABHIK BHANU

PARTRIDGE
A Penguin Company

ISBN: Hardcover   978-1-4828-1055-4
               Softcover   978-1-4828-1056-1
               Ebook   978-1-4828-1054-7

Partridge books may be ordered through booksellers or by contacting:

Partridge India
Penguin Books India Pvt.Ltd
11, Community Centre, Panchsheel Park, New Delhi 110017
India
www.partridgepublishing.com
Phone: 000.800.10062.62

Thank you . . .

. . . Dr. R.K. Anand being my mentor, Rajendra Gandhi, Rajmohan Gandhi and Tripurari Saran inspired me to stand with honesty, truthfulness, everyone at Panchgani who are silently building towards a great India.

. . . My Grandma who first taught me about Mahatma Gandhi and Bhaiya my first school of learning life.

. . . Appu Bhaiya who always stood by me whenever I needed him, someone who trusted my talent as film maker and writer.

. . . Dharam Vakhariya and George Thomas being my first professional school at Mumbai.

. . . Sudhanshu Jena, a friend in a true sense.

. . . Anurag Agarwal of Arya College Jaipur, a man of the time, who inspired me to dare challenges.

. . . Painter, poet, actor Akanksha, whose smile and designs both matter a lot.

. . . And life is incomplete without Pradeep Katiyar & Lalla whom I love from the core of my heart.

. . . Verma aunty, Shiva (Chinto), Anup and family my 1st shelter . . .

. . . Nitesh Banker for reposing trust in me . . . .

. . . Susanna Jans who knows what friendship means.

. . . Chandra Pandula, our great Krishna connection . . .

. . . Shekhar ji, whose a kind man whom I love to convey my work.

. . . Peter, whom I always remember as best classmate.

. . . Symbiosis college, my first platform of life.

. . . Mrs. Ashok Mehta who is always ready to support good cause.

. . . Naina,Sunil, Angad , Ashok, and Malay for being with me.

. . . Last, but not the least, how can I forget Pinku Biswas, Gaurav Govind (Babbu), Sheela Srivastava, B.N. Tiwari, Atul, Anirudh Kumar, Govind Dada, Anju, Keshav, Ranjana, Tiya, Ridhi, Suchi, Sneha, Rajita, Siddhant, Parag Deasi, Khushboo, Vineet, Ranjana, Manoj, and many generation next . . .

Dedicated to
Madan Mohan Prasad,
Annapurna Prasad,
Sushama Khare,
Yogendra Bahadur Khare.

1

'This dame is in love!'

Jyotika let the voice pass over. She knows, the boy standing close to her has passed this comment. She is standing at the corner of the lane connected to Prithvi theatre. He has actually said 'excuse me' asking her to shift, so that he shouldn't be blamed for brushing his shoulder to her, which he did. Glanced at her with a sarcastic smile and walked away. It happens in a place like this country, where female feticide and infanticide is a normal phenomenon. It is difficult to analyze, whether women are worshiped, neglected or insulted here, in this nation. At times, she becomes upset while thinking on these issues, especially when she is pissed off, waiting for her boyfriend, Ray. Otherwise, she is least concerned about these topics.

The dried muddy soil has bore solidified effect, looking cement-hard. It is hard to say whether the land has swallowed the previous cement porch or, the bricks have fit themselves in the soil to give a different look to the surface. Normally nowadays, the tiles or marbles are used to make the surface look beautiful, however, this strange pattern has emerged naturally.

A very big movie star has started Prithvi theatre in his father's name. The theatre is known for promoting theatre culture. It's Ray's favorite place. The small campus has trees surrounded by solid bricks to protect the roots, which also make the place look like 'Never seen this kind of place . . .' impression to the visitors. A canteen which serves tea, coffee and snacks with self service, crowd enriching the place by claiming themselves intellectuals, poets, writers, artistes make their presence with pride, having their heads held high.

It can't be red, off red, maroon type color faded to help the impact it has into demoralizing the boundary wall.

Which has helped creating a book stall so that literature can be sold, if not sold at least promoted and marketed to the world where electronic media has taken over; and is killing the readership. She noticed that the book seller is bored having monotonous ambience. Girls showing legs and sleeves is a motivating factor at times, but that is also droning after a point. When he wants tea, he orders a 'cutting chai' (half cup of tea) from the tea stall standing outside the Prithvi premises, as he can't afford tea from the Prithvi's tea stall. He doesn't understand the logic behind people preferring tea or coffee without milk, while enjoying the play or passing time sitting in at a small cafeteria at Juhu. The bitter taste of coffee gives a vomiting tendency, once he tasted and felt like taking out the entire stomach content, it was really nauseating. Tea with lots of milk and sugar is real fun to have, after every two hours. He knows the artist kind of people are known as different creatures who love to be treated differently. Their attitude reveals themselves as profound intellectuals with long beard and long hair, bizarre costume, smoking and projecting themselves as 'lived my life, know more than anyone else, not interested kind of attitude etc. 'Prithvi is the hub of these geniuses, who are ready to reject any talent which exists.

Jyotika noticed the book seller looking at her, he might be thinking she is a fool waiting for another fool. She hates this kind of moment where she is made to give importance to some one, thinking about a person who is foolish, whose name is Ray, her guy whom she thinks hard and tries to make some decision whether or not she should entertain him any further.

However, she doesn't notice anything when Ray is in her mind, she doesn't see anyone but him, she doesn't miss anyone, but him. This guy has changed her life . . . She is waiting for her guy, standing outside the theatre. The show is about to begin and Ray is seen nowhere. She feels lost, looking for Ray, the boy passing the comment is so right . . . She is really in love. The moment she accepts that she loves someone, the very next moment she refuses it. Love is a state of mind like the way happiness is; and Jyotika wants to know the status of her mind, asking herself whether or not she is in love?

'Love is the strongest emotion . . . some emotions are perishable, like hate is an emotion too, which can't stand for quite a long time, but love does.' Ray said one day.

The truth is, she doesn't want to confess that she is in love. Thinking of someone and wanting to be with someone can be called love. She has to take the decision one day sooner or later. Moment of friction becomes precious, when you are in a dilemma, whether you are in love with someone or not. When the difficult time comes, to confess to yourself that, yes! I love this person; then, that decision makes you or breaks you.

'The decisions are based on your memory chips, memory chips store information, experiences. Naturally not necessarily, the decision we make is right, which is always based on facts we know. As we know limited facts, our decisions also have limitations.' Ray has explained once, comprehending her entire thought process.

'. . .But people do make decision to live life.' Jyotika objected.

'Yes, and their decisions do go wrong.' Ray was instant. Ray is different. She knows. Yes! She can be sure about her guy.

Jyotika has to choose one between the two - Ray and Sunny . . . Sunny, unlike Ray is a successful business tycoon. He is so calm, cool and he hardly talks to her. He is silent most of the times, very shy, thoughtful and unexpressive. And most importantly, he is never a late comer like Ray.

The play has begun and there is no sign of Ray. She feels really stupid waiting for Ray every time. And this time, she decides not to call him, just wait for another 5 minutes and leave. She had actually told herself that she will wait till the play begins.

This happens when you love someone. Sunny always comes in time and waits for her sitting on stairs, till the time she comes. Is it because Sunny loves her, and Ray doesn't? What nonsense! Love does not depend on if someone is late or not. It's such a stupid thought! . . .These thoughts must rest, at least for a while! She buys a cup of coffee and sits on one of the tile benches arranged under a green tree. Amazing place! Ray always selects open places, full of nature. Small, cool and calm. People have gone inside and have started watching the play, the play which she was supposed to watch!! 'Oh shit!' the coffee cup kept on the edge of the wooden bench falls down. She takes some tissue papers to save her skirt from getting stained. The waiter arrives promptly and cleans the place. Jyotika is irritated with herself, what an idiot I am! waiting for last 45 minutes, why? . . . She looks down at her purse and finds a folded newspaper peeping out, she opens the newspaper . . . Oh, it's a poem! Ray's poem published in the newspaper and he had kept it just like this. She smiles, not a bad idea, to kill time -

MY KITE

I fly my kite in sky
When it rains . . .
Only . . . when it rains.
My Kite leaves the surface . . .
Goes up.
loves the height
That's what my kite is like.
I whistle when it touches the sky.
I fly my kite in sky
When it rains . . .
Only, when it rains.

She knows he is genius, a real genius. She smiles reading those lines, reads the few lines again - that's what my kite is like, I whistle when it touches the sky . . . She senses a known fragrance, the one she always feels when Ray is with her. She tilts her chin up, sees him standing in front of her, smiling. When did he come? She suddenly realizes, he is late. She should be angry.

'What is this Ray!'

'What?' Ray was cool with a smile on his face.

'You are late, very late . . .'

'Ya, I think so.'

'You think so? Why are you late?'

'Come on buddy, it happens! Do you really wanna know why I'm so late?

'Yes. Tell me.'

'I wanted you to wait and think of that person, whom you are waiting for. So I made you think about me. I will have a cup of coffee, do you want one? . . . Oh! You had already! I think the soil had some coffee too. As usual, you must have spilled over here.'

'Do not deviate, I want an honest answer.'

'Honest answer? Ok! I was sleeping, I got up late. You know how I am!' Ray goes to the coffee counter, she keeps watching him at the coffee counter placing order for coffee.

She knows, she can't fight with him, she can't spoil the moments she spends with him. She realizes she is very happy when she sees him. Blue loose jeans, white loose T shirt, floaters in his feet, a casual approach, a cool guy, what's special in this boy? Why she has fallen in love with him? She is surprised at her own self, thinking whether or not she should be.

Ray, is a ray of her life.

She met Ray for the first time, when it was raining. She was waiting for her car to come from the packed traffic venue,

'Ex happiness' she still remembers the name of the play. She noticed a boy trying to get an auto-rickshaw. He was wet.

'Are you looking for a rick?' She didn't know why did she ask so, suddenly looking at him, unknown to the fact that, that question will change her life.

'Ya,' he replied in short, looking at her with a surprise and concern, and wants to know why she is suddenly interested in someone who has no mode of communication, not even a cell phone. A girl, not beautiful, not an extraordinary stunning beautiful girl wearing navy blue skirt and red sleeveless top asking her for a lift, he thought so.

'Want to share a rick with me?' Ray asked.

'I have my car, coming.' She replied with a little smile.

'Oh . . . Good!' Ray is always like that, as if he wasn't quite much impressed.

'I can drop you at your place if you want.' She offered him a lift . . . But why? . . . to a stranger? . . . Sometimes in life things happen just like that . . .for no reason . . .or they happen because they were pre-decided, may be. May be she was destined to meet him like that.

'I am going to Bandra, what about you?' Ray asked.

'Worli!'

'But there should be a car if you wanna drop someone?' Either he is sarcastic or he is not believing her, that's what she was thinking, by the time the car arrived. She entered the expensive car and so did he, following her. He was not impressed at all. He was happy, he got mode of commutation to reach home.

He was very talkative, kept talking about his mom, who was waiting for him and might be worried. And that he hates to keep cell phone, so cannot communicate at home.

'You can make a call from my cell,' she offered. He called his mom and briefed her that he will be there in some time. She didn't know that, a 'lift to a stranger like him' would change her life. Meeting people is very important, you meet many but remember few and make friends with very few. Life is so unpredictable. It is full of surprises. And today, she can't live without Ray. He is there with her every moment, even he is in her dreams when she is asleep.

Ray has finished his coffee and is enjoying being silent.

'I love the moment when we sit together in silence and say nothing.' Only Ray can say that. He loves being with his girlfriend with no conversation. Amazing thought!

'We converse even if we do not speak.' Ray had said this when Jyotika complained of him for not speaking. A relaxed mind, great sense of humor, ready to crack jokes any time in any situations, that's what Ray is, that's what he tries to be always.

'What's the point, you are hardly speaking.' She wanted him to converse.

'If you and me are not talking, we understand the words of silence, I see in your eyes and you blush.' Ray had said with a smile. He was so right . . . They smile looking at each other, asking what next? . . . Smile, and what next? It always ends with kisses. Both of them make themselves 'love birds' in open restaurant.

'Love is the only feeling which relaxes you and gives power to live more,' Ray made a final and authoritative comment.

'Tell me one thing Ray. How are you so confident, when you say all these things?' Jyotika asked.

'I say these things only because I am confident. There is no point in saying something, when you are not sure about it.' Ray has a reply for everything as usual; and most of the time he is right.

Yes! It's only she, who thinks he is right, and not her parents. According to them, their daughter is in love with a boy who doesn't care for life. Isn't she making a mistake being with a guy like Ray, who isn't serious about life. He is just interested in composing music, writing lyrics with his team and claiming that Rainbow will be heard worldwide. She is confused whom to choose, she likes Ray and her family likes her childhood friend Sunny.

'Ray is a magician!' She claims.

'Ray? He is an idiot, he thinks he is smart, over smart!' Her dad thinks exactly opposite, 'He is good for nothing, he knows I am rich and you are my only daughter.'

'Look at Sunny, he has started from scratch. He didn't take a single penny from his Dad, he has reached to the top, dealing with hundreds of millions.' Charu adds.

'I have seen life, I know what life is!' Dad says.

'Age is a number, one who claims intellect on the basis of years passed is simply exaggeration, it's not the same situation we face like what our older generation has faced.' Ray explains it.

'Your dad is a slave of situations. He enjoys being a slave of money, rituals, tradition. He needs some fresh air with fresh thoughts,' Ray says with smile. 'He needs a treatment as he is sick!'

How dare he call my dad a slave and sick; Jyotika's first thought was aggressive. Very aggressive! In fact she was sick and tired of his comments like this. She was disturbed and upset. She didn't meet him next day at least to show that she didn't like someone calling her dad a slave, sick and all these bad things.

'Why would someone call anyone slave? My dad works for family. He is a rich man! And being a rich man does not mean being a slave, what rubbish! Ray doesn't know how tough it is to pay salaries to many staff members at the end of the month. And what does he do? Being lazy and doing nothing instead writing poems, composing music . . . 'Music is my world' so he is also a slave of music . . . slave! My foot!!'

The whole world knows Ray is lazy.

2

*R*ay's thoughts are taking away Jyotika's peace of mind. Jyotika doesn't know what her mind is up to? She is occupied with Ray's thoughts 24x7, whether she is with him, without him.

At home, with mom, stirring spoon in the bowl, overhearing her mom's instructions,

'Eat baby finish it fast, do you want pulses? It has protein, you have not touched the soup, sip it hot, it's very tasty, what are you doing? Where are you lost?'

Ray is clear about one thing, that, he wants to be a free soul. He doesn't want to complicate issues. He thinks that, life may be very simple, but people complicate it unnecessarily. Futile exercises suck him. Why to carry extra baggage, not required in the journey of life? If someone decides to reach east and heads to east, he will achieve reaching east; but in most of the cases, one thinks of reaching east and heads to west, and then blames the destiny, for not reaching east.

Ray says happiness is the concept that confuses those who attempt to have it. He is sure about one thing that, the search for happiness is futile unless one doesn't make others happy, simple concept! People do not understand it. Do they? Why can't he be simple and normal like others, follow established norms. Life will be easy going, no hotchpotch of these mind boggling theories, searching happiness, love and life, without discovering the world!

'It's a slaves' world. A chase race in competitive motion which provokes one to prove to others that he is better than rest of the world. So, be my slave, follow my orders. One becomes slave himself in this process of trying to make others, his slaves'. The game goes on and on like a chess . . .the gambit! One step here one step there, that's it! That's how it is! And the game is on forever. Life anyway is nothing but eating, shitting sleeping, sleeping alone or with someone else! Some adventure, a bit of jealousy, tint of love, partial hate and finally death! A journey of 100 years, is just to look for meaning, or what else?'

Ray rumbles: 'A blind thinks that he would see everything once he gets eyes, but can he really?'

'Love helps to find meaning in life'. He wants to discover the word 'love' to know what love is?
'When one becomes emotional and for someone having been in his or her company make a claim of love for each other, that's love', he says.

He kept throwing his weighty lectures, adding boring flavours to it. She refused to take it one day, when it was enough.
'Only beast like you can make a rubbish statement like that'. Jyotika differed and made one statement in response to all, she knew he will fall flat.

'If I stay with a dog for a longer time, I will start loving it, you meant this?' She was listening for a long time, long lectures of someone who claims to be her love, so called love, if he may know a meaning of 'love' that is very simple, everyone knows it except Ray the arrogant foolish, a philosopher, discovering love!

'Actually yes, forget dog, one can fall in love with your musical instrument, study table, and many things just because they are around us always.'
'We fall in love and have sex with them right?'

'I meant love and not sex!' She loaded off her thoughts in front of Ray, no point in talking to him, he can make people believe anything. Their love is an emotion because they spent time together, that is what he meant by saying that.

He has his own way to express his love. He is causal in his relationships, talks loud and straight. Some understand it others misunderstand! He has his typical mannerisms to express his feelings.

Music is the love of his life. 'Rainbow' is his dream, a mission for which one life is short. Music makes him realize that he utilizes his moments of life . . .this thought keeps him alive. Ray wants to investigate the meaning of success and at the same time he doesn't evade from the fact that, why success is very important in life that everyone is chasing it at any cost, by hook or crook.

Ray hardly reads. He thinks knowledge is his power, when he is with Jyotika, he is rowdy. When he touches Jyotika, his forceful possessive acts turn into physical fight between them, Jyotika pores a bucket full of water many a times when she finds him sleeping. Many a times the cushion gets wet and Menka shouts at them as who has done that. Ray chases to catch her having wet cloth and Jyotika hides behind Menka.

'You both would fall one day,' says Menka.
'You will break your own bones for sure and I am not going to take you guys to hospital.' They keep on jumping on the floor running chasing Jyotika. Menka has accepted these childish fake war between them by now.

Jyotika loves being at Ray's home till late night many times. Avoiding many calls made by her mom. She wants Ray to be with her all the time which Ray doesn't. Ray is moody he wants fun while playing with her body and when he is saturated he would play music and ask her to listen his poetry, ask her to bring something sometimes glass of water or make tea or hold some musical instrument with warning that the musical instrument shouldn't be spoilt. Many a times she gets confused as he treats her like a toy and she refuses to be his toy, no way.

She is Jyotika and no one dictates terms on her, not even her boyfriend. And hold on for a while, who is her boyfriend? No one! Ray is a boyfriend or not, yet to be decided. Her mind swings with changing thoughts. Just because she spends time with Ray he doesn't become her boyfriend. He may be a close friend like many others and she is always with him in presence of Menka so it's fine! And why she loves to spend much time with him? Only because of infatuation for him and these physical touches like kissing, hugging are nothing but friendly touches. In a close friend's company one may have such fun moments, so not a big deal. Not a deal like 'life partner,' no, not at all!

She rejects all her own possessive ideas! Those idiotic ideas like Ray being someone so close, that it seems to be a strong, solid decision, boyfriend first and hubby later! Not now, it's too early. She will take a decision but not so early. He is not a suitable boy, lazy and just lethargic, late comer, good for nothing, 'He' is just not working! Life's decisions are to be taken with lots of care. She is careful and she will decide such important things with extra care, not in haste.

He is damn smart. He has mesmerized her, she can't see the real picture, can't see anyone, can't go anywhere. He is a black magician and not musician. He impresses her with his poems. Next time she won't listen to his poems, yes! There! She gets involved when she hears some creative crap, that's the crux of the magic. He has magic in his words and music . . .next time onwards, she wouldn't listen to any music also. That's the smart trap he has. She should avoid meeting him also. He never keeps time commitments. Just imagine someone who doesn't call his girlfriend these days! It's always she, who has to make calls to him. Forget about calling, he doesn't even keep a cell. She gets many sweet messages from many, but him.

And what rubbish excuse he has . . .

'I do not keep cell, it is nuisance.' What nonsense! Everyone keeps cell, today no one is so backward like him.

'When you have many thoughts and unable to arrive at a decision, relax, get out from that thought for time being and do something else; you will find a solution at one point when you omit thinking about it.' Ray advised once.

She loves recalling what Ray says time and again. And she remembers what he said that day, when they were riding on elephant. Matheran trip! They had driven down to Matheran, the man who owned elephant, offered them ride. Only Rs 200! He had offered the ride against some money and she and Ray had the opportunity for that ride. It was really great experience. She enjoyed the stupid ride on the top of an elephant with Ray because Ray was also with her. It was fantastic and with lots of romance. He was hugging her tight from back. She felt his touch full of love. Their bodies were shaking. The Mahvat was feeling shy, seeing such bold romance of Ray. Ray doesn't bother where he is, he would hold tight and kiss her at any place. She doesn't dislike it, but there should be some decency when you are kissing your love!

But why the hell is she thinking of him? That's the problem when you fall in love with someone. You can't escape from thinking about that fellow, whether you like it or not. There is absolutely no control at all on oneself. And her case is so different, she is not sure about anything and love! For sure she is not in love with this guy. And why she is thinking about him? She is not thinking but recalling some incidents, so that she can make some correct decisions! She makes herself understand this, before going to the bed. And makes sure that she should tell herself million times that Ray is bad, very bad, when she gets up every morning. That would help for sure.

3

Sunny tries calling Jyotika next morning.

As usual her phone is switched off. He went her home.

'She is sleeping, go wake her up!' Charu wants Jyotika to keep meeting Sunny. She wants Sunny to become their son- in- law, not Ray.

Sunny moves to wake her up. He liked the idea to see Jyotika sleeping less covered.

He enters the bedroom, the bed is full of teddy bears and pillows, she is in deep sleep, looking awesomely sensuous, milky fair legs are smooth shining, sleeveless shoulders, deep free cleavage tells a story of carefree millionaire girl who doesn't care for anything, loves just being herself at her mood and listens and guided absolutely by her mood and tantrums. Everyone bows to that. His girl?. Yes, of course his girl, there are rumors she is seeing someone. He left everything to prove that it's just a rumor and no truth in it. She is his 'would be wife', would be his wife very soon. For sure. A shadow of sunlight touching her face as the direct sun is not able to enter the window of her bedroom, the room has been structured in a way or may be the position of the bed is in a certain way. He tries to understand the architecture of the bed room, he might have visited it a couple of times with Jyotika, but never noticed that. Indeed an ideal ventilated room for fresh air.

'What are you doing here? Can't you see I am sleeping?'

'I was asked to wake you up, I am just following the orders, your cell is switched off. I am here to take you for a drive, do not say 'NO' now.'

Great, that's really is great! I will go with him, as it is I am fed up of Ray, that may be a good escape to be away from Ray. It would help. Space in a relationship certainly works. She knows and believes having space for time being when it is complicated. Has her relationship been complicated? No it hasn't, it needs introspection for betterment. May be she is trying to be sure from these fluctuating wavering thoughts. Not a bad idea to be away from Ray and to be with Sunny who cares so much.

Sunny is always happy to be with her. He has taken an off from his work. They went for a long drive. He took her to Panchgani. Sunny is a gentleman, a thorough gentleman! He is disciplined, very caring. He has attended almost every small and big event organized by both the families till date. Jyotika's parents think that, Sunny is a suitable match for her, as he is elder to her and according to the old Indian customs it suits well, one who is elder and matured, takes right decision when required!

Sunny never uses foul language. He is decent.

On phone he lets Jyotika talk more and he plays role of a listener, so that he can pay more attention to her. He wears formals. He is tall, with stalwart looks, having a little muscular body and does a bit of work out regularly, every morning. So good, a great choice! Be it! Let him suffer! Let Ray suffer who has no respect for his beautiful girl.

Sunny's mother expired when he was very young, he lives with his servant Miraj since then. He and his Dad live close to Jyotika's bungalow, near Worli sea face. He loves Jyotika, she knows it but he has never expressed his love. 'Strawberries!', he stops his car and bought some. 'Aunty loves them!' Sunny is a family person, he loves to talk about everyone, even Miraj, who is his care taker after his mom's demise. 'Take it' Jyotika smiled, Ray is in her thoughts. She has to ignore Ray related thoughts. She can't think of Ray. She knows Ray wouldn't call. Ray is either sleeping, or he must have gone to his music team. Why is she bothered? Be it. Let him go anywhere he likes, any part of the world. Not her problem.

'I often come to see this place.' Sunny stopped the car to show her a resort type big bungalow, surrounded by hills; and there is water flowing down the valley.

'I have recently bought this place.' Sunny tried to surprise her bringing at a place like this. Did he? Could he? Does she feel surprised?

'I find it very peaceful here, which I feel nowhere.' Sunny extended his show.

Ray has nothing, he cannot commit for a single thing, he is not sure in life. He writes lyrics, composes music and lives completely free from dreaming any materialistic achievements. On the other hand, Sunny has everything, properties, business, trade, commitment and a planned life. And most important, Sunny loves her since childhood. Then why she is always happy when she is with Ray?

'Happiness is an emotion of a momentum. It goes, as it comes.' Ray says.

A guy who takes life lightly, for him everything is defined, can't be her love of life. She is convinced about this thought.

Life is life! How can one take it so lightly! Ray doesn't even know how to touch a girl, he offers a rusty, rowdy touch, whenever he kisses me, it's so passionate that . . . forget it! She is with Sunny and should be with him only.

'Life is a traveling of many years and every moment of the journey is important. Success and failure rate your standing and, outstanding.' Ray smiles when he explains his perspective about life. Ray's vision towards life is completely different.

'But, a sensible girl will choose Sunny, not Ray, only an idiot like her can fall in love with a stupid boy like him.' Jyotika can't ignore thinking about Ray.

She should think of Sunny.

'Sunny is successful, caring, good looking, tall and handsome, like any girl's dream man. On the contrary, Ray would be rejected on his very first date, when he would arrive late. And he should be further rejected when he would say, 'life is a futile exercise for nothing and love is a perishable emotion!' No girl can accept this rubbish thought, except me! What he thinks of himself? Hasn't made a single call, and why should she call him all the time? Who is he? My boss? He should also call me, both of us love each other! Why then she advocates Ray? Is she foolish? Really? And who is he? Looking at his bizarre dress sense, how does he wear his clothes! Loose T shirts, baggy pants, lost personality! He takes his legs up on the seat, knees folded while he watches movie. Only an idiot like her will tolerate him else who is so stupid in this entire world? She knows she is trying to find reason to hate him, she knows, she can't. She would end up loving him at the end of the day . . .

'Let's walk on the hills.' Sunny makes an announcement.

'Shush!' Jyotika wants to silence him. Her thoughts were still lingering around Ray. Let me get rid of Ray first. She doesn't want this guy. She has been pissed off having been occupied with the thoughts of Ray. This love crap sucks her, why the hell she is in love with someone like him, why? One who doesn't even deserve my friendship. This creature called Ray has reached at the core of my head.

Both of them are walking on the hills. 'Awesome place!' She feels the soothing cold breeze. Soothing climate. What a place! Sunny is no doubt an amazing person. He has definitely a taste for fantastic places like this. He should have been a right choice, then what is she waiting for? For whom? Why can't she be happy with Sunny, with whom she has come to Panchgani, may be on a date . . .

Jyotika's chain of thoughts is still getting longer and longer. Lunch was ready by the time they got back after the walk. The caretaker of the bungalow has managed everything in time as instructed by Sunny. Salad, non spicy healthy food. The table was full of vegetarian dishes. Sunny is a vegetarian. This is the only thing which she doesn't like about him. She loves non-vegetarian food. He knows this, he should have organized for some non-veg food.

The very next moment, she notices a dish full of fish cuisines kept for her. 'They managed to organize Pomfret only,' Sunny says with a smile, having salad in his mouth. She should marry this guy just for this! Jyotika is really impressed by his hospitality.

'You don't eat fish but!'

'So what? It's your personal choice. I must take care of that as you are my . . .' He stops saying something and pretends that he is eating something.

'Fish is really tasty. Who made this? I must thank him.' Sunny looked at the person who was serving.

'Call Patil!' Patil comes ahead quickly.

'My wife made it. It's not from the sea. We go early in the morning to get it, there, down the water. I can bring you some prawns tomorrow,' Patil was very excited.

'We are not here for tomorrow but next time definitely.' Sunny concludes.

'Thanks for making such delicious food.' Jyotika concluded.

The car is talking to the air of Panchgani. Jyotika is silent. Sunny is also silent . . . Everything, yet something is missing. Again, she is thinking of Ray.

She shouldn't. He is her would be husband. All the problems of life will be sorted out. He will take tensions and she would enjoy life. They would visit France, Los Angeles, Stuttgart, Australia and Panchgani together. They would have babies. They would call the Rainbow band to play music. Ray would dance or play music. This seemed not a very bad idea at all. She would ask him, order him to play Rainbow song. He and his team Bosky, Joy, Mac, Shubh, Reheman all of them will play Rainbow . . .

Rainbow . . .
I love rainbow
Life is unknown
Unknown moments
Drop we gain
Water again again . . .
Rain rain and rain . . .
Rainbow Rainbow I love rainbow . . .

She, her husband Sunny and their kids would enjoy listing to this music. Ray has written the song . . . What amazing lines, wonderful!! Awesome group of musicians!'

'You guys are magicians!' she complemented all of them the other day, when she had visited them for the first time.

Sunny stops the car for taking a break. Evening has arrived with orange floss in the sky. Sun is going down. She is standing close to the car with a cup of tea. People around them are looking at Sunny who is asking for mineral water and the 12 year boy unable to understand him. Sunny buys a water bottle and comes close to the car. He looks at her, smiles. Jyotika sets her hair and smiles too.

'Ray calls it a magic light.' Jyotika begins the conversation.

'Who is Ray?' Sunny asked.

'A very close friend of mine. My best friend!'

'Oh! Never heard from you.'

'Ya, we just met; around five months back, but we kind of get along very often.'

Ohh! . . . He must be someone really interesting who has come so close so fast.'

'Yes, he is.'

'So how did you meet him?'

'I offered him lift in my car while it was raining cats and dogs, one night.'

'He doesn't have a car?'

'Yeh! He uses public transport.'

Silence for some time.

'So what you were doing then?' He is jealous, and being sarcastic.

'I was watching 'Ex happiness' alone. No friend was interested watching that play at Prithvi.'

'It's John Oscar's film, right?'

'It's a play, not a film.'

'Ya, I have heard about it. How is it?'

'Its one a kind of a play! Ray watches these kind of plays. I was waiting for my car, he was searching for a rick.' Sunny is surprised. What a girl! She had given lift to someone unknown, stupid girl!

The car again starts running on the road. Jyotika wants to talk about Ray and his team, his music and all. She keeps on talking without taking a single breath.

'Ray is a very talented poet, lyricist, music director, he is just fantastic! You know, his team is . . . I can't explain . . . Joy, Bosky, Manoj, Rehman, Vendy, everyone! You know Sunny, they didn't have place to practice, they found out some shelter on the hills, Pali Hills! That place belonged to a big builder. When he came to know that a musical band has occupied it and had almost encroached on the place, without permission, he was very angry.'

'But Ray was cool, he told Khan, that builder, to relax and just listen to the song . . .' She explains in excitement as if it is happening in front of her.

'. . . I tell you Sunny, you wouldn't believe that, when Ray played the Rainbow song, the builder was mesmerized listening to the music of Rainbow. He hugged Ray and his team and said, 'This is your place. Do whatever you want to and tell me if you need any financial help'. She paused for a moment.

'Can you believe this Sunny, today the builder Khan is their investor! Ray is different. He is very creative. His only bad habit is laziness. He is not punctual also. He wears loose T shirt and baggy trousers and he is . . . he is very careless, keeps forgetting things. But otherwise he is gem of a person. He writes very well. Ray defines life in one line.' The car is going fast, faster.

Sunny is listening calmly with patience!

4

Sunny reached home very late.

He was very tired, not because he drove several miles alone having preferded to drive without a driver to have private moment with Jyotika, where two of them can feel more than talk.

The mind eludes chaotic events of the day which grips his nerves to a sign and indication that she may be no more 'his girl' which, he is not ready to accept making argument with himself, 'too early to say', 'she is just seeing him'. His mind war is bringing in many facts 'see this' 'see that' 'she said this, she didn't say that' she was mentally absent while being with him. It was his outing, dominated by Ray's conversation. His awe was present without his presence, that's Sunny nerves declining and refusing against his contention in the throbbing debate of his nerves. Ray gains more points than him in the debate of his own mind and that made him tired and not the 400 miles driving.

He was quiet and upset, when he heard that Jyotika is seeing someone called 'Ray'. He pretended that he doesn't know any creature called 'Ray'. He had heard the so called 'creative guy' trying to take away Jyotika, his childhood love from him. Rumor, wasn't a rumor at all. Ray is challenging his childhood love effortlessly.

'This guy is acting oversmart, that's it!' Pratap uncle explained in front of everyone last night when Jyotika came very late. Everyone is unhappy about the fact that, Jyotika being friendly with Ray and his band group. Pratap uncle clearly instigated him reminding his duties towards his would be wife being encroached by someone else.

'The sale would be finished in a few more days, hurry!' It sounded alarming like this- 'Do something, be a man, not a dud.' Pratap uncle told vehemently challenging him to get up from his kip.

He planned the Panchgani trip immediately without a moment's delay, made several calls to her cell, which was switched off. He had a long shower.

The question is whether he can win Jyotika over Ray? They want him to win. He finds that he is losing his ground. That pinches him. Is this guy so powerful?

He knows having a shower is not the solution of the problem, his mind's hurricane needs serenity. He opens all the windows of the top floor of his three storied bungalow. He allows the wind to blow and whirl in the room. The clean shining off white marbles are imported from Europe mostly from France. He loves to be unique in every sense, his room should be clean, things should be properly placed at their places. Absolute professionalism. No hanky panky business.

Closing his eyes, he starts breathing slowly and deeply.

He has got his room made fully ventilated. He closes his eyes breathing in and breathing out. The soothing mantra logan music is on. The thought is bothering him, 'Ray is amazing, Rainbow. He has great team of musicians. It's ok! People could be good but how can Jyotika choose someone instead of Sunny. His stress is not easing.'

The meditation is also not helping him today. Meditating is the best treatment when mind is occupied with so many complicated thoughts. But the meditation requires lots of patience and practice. How the hell one can concentrate, when his girlfriend is seeing someone else. He knows not even God, but what would give him quick repose -Vodka! Vodka may help him, or may be Champagne, little Champagne! He is right! Vodka captures his imagination. Probably for sometime.

Jyotika likes Ray, may be? He has entered in her life, has succeeded in impressing her, these things are temporary and will pass over soon. It's a matter of time. How can she do this to him? He loves her. She should know that, she knows that, he might have made a mistake by not proposing her, but is any formal proposal needed? He doesn't believe in all this stupid crap. She knows that he loves her, the entire world knows, his family knows, her parents want her to get married to him. What if it doesn't happen? She, the one in a million would leave him with millions of assets! Not possible, he wouldn't let it happen.

He had never ever thought of any girl in his life, except her. It's not possible. Nothing is impossible, anything can happen, Life is unpredictable and once you expect something to happen, he should be prepared for the worst, Jyotika might leave him.

All his life he worked hard to see his happiness with Jyotika, he finds suddenly, he has lost meaning for his success. His mother expired when he was very young. His dad was busy setting up his new business in city like Mumbai. His dad had come from Delhi and settled down at Worli sea face with the help of Jyotika's Dad. After the death of his mom his Dad never got married. Sunny was shy from childhood. He has worked hard to reach this successful position. He knows that at the end of the day whatever people talk, what matters is success, money and lavish lifestyle. People do not respect to one does not have money.

'Your mom was a very different lady . . .' His dad use to say. 'She was calm and cool in every situation, very kind, always loved reading and discussing what life is . . . Fortunately, she had lots of time for these things, because I was busy all the time in business.'

He knows he can't find a lady like his mom may be that's the reason he never tried even once to marry any other woman. She is always with me in my thoughts and in my dreams, I know only one lady in life and she was so complete that I never needed to think of anyone, the beauty, elegance and power of trust . . . She was full of positive energy. No matter how tired I was her one smile was enough to ease me.

Yes, he knows one right girl and life is on the perfect track with positive energy. Jyotika is that kind of energy, like her mom. Is she or isn't she? Everyone is different from one another. We all are human beings, we all think and act differently. He loves Jyotika. The matter of fact is she loves him too. He thinks so . . . May be, actually she was in love with him but not any more now, so is it too late? Has he lost her as girlfriend? He has to now take care and see that Jyotika comes back in his life again. She is his girl, they know each other for years now. This guy what is his name? . . . Yes, Ray has just come . . . and would go as he has come. He is sure. But does time matter? In love does time matter? What if she doesn't come back? What if she . . . she would or wouldn't she?

What is he thinking? She will have to, his love is not like any Tom, Dick and Harry. Nobody can just take her away. He is not just standing on road selling peanuts, he is an industrialist a self made business tycoon, whose products own nation wide reputation.

Sunny starts comparing Ray and himself, he feels so disturbed, occupied with stupid thoughts. He can't concentrate on anything. He looks outside at the sea . . . the street light is shining and reflection of the light in the sea is making it look beautiful. What's God's creation. His mind is reeling the thoughts of Ray and Jyotika.

This guy is creative, Ray is creative.

Jyotika loves him because he writes, he has written Rainbow songs she was humming. She was totally zapped with his thoughts when they were coming back. It's 2 am in the morning. He couldn't sleep, watching Jyotika's photos, He knows something is bothering him . . . Jyotika's guy. He is insecure, he is a musician and such people can impress anyone, even he loves some of them, when Jyotika listens to Ray's songs she goes mad. Sitar, Violin, Guitar, even he loves music and let's lose himself when some one plays these instrument.

He felt like calling Koyal. Koyal, joined him when he started the company, ever since then, she had been very big support. Koyal is the solution of all problems, all company's problems. She is full of positive energy. Koyal has been the solution for company's every problem.

Initially, the company was not doing well, but they never compromised with quality, both of them decided to maintain the quality instead of aggressive marketing. Koyal really worked hard with Sunny. Koyal joined hands with Sunny as friend as well as an investor. Her father invested his hard earned money in the company and today both are happy to see it as a nationally reputed brand!

He spent maximum time during those years to build the reputation and brand and may be Jyotika has been taken for granted since that time. She was in the second year of graduation. He is elder to Jyotika by around five years. Quite an age difference. Is this happening because of the age gap? Doesn't he belong to the same age group? Does Ray belong to in her age group? Sunny remembers she used to call a lot, yes but he always responded back to all his calls. He revived all those years, days, hours, minutes and seconds. Where did he make mistake? Did he? What went wrong? He has taken a long breath. He, in no way can afford to lose her. He loves her. Jyotika is his love of life. Without Jyotika life is empty and meaningless, it's not life just days, hours, minutes, seconds . . .

5

*J*yotika woke up late.

'What's the time?' She asked her mom, who had come to wake her up.

'It's time to get up, wake up Jyotika.' Her mom was sitting right besides her, looking at her face with affection. Jyotika opened her eyes, hugged her mom, and slept again, keeping her head on her mom's lap. Her mom smiled and moved her lap. Suddenly her head fell on the bed. Jyotika realized that, she knew what her mom is up to. She didn't let her mom go just like that. She again caught her mom, and fixed her head on her mom's lap with hands around her waist. This time her mom had no chance to move her body.

Their daughter-mother relationship was strong. Her mother was a very simple cool lady. She always teased her by calling her, 'cool mom!'

She looked the same in all dresses but jeans and T shirt suited her a lot. The three of them were always surrounded by drivers, servants, gardeners and security guards, furniture and stress. Having a bungalow at a place like 'Worli sea face' was a sign of a rich man in the city of Mumbai.

'I am going for shopping, are you coming?' Charu knew she would never refuse for shopping.

'I have to go to meet Ray for his music band 'Jyotika jumps up from the bed and entered in the bathroom. Her mom just looked at her but didn't say anything.

'Shit! I am late.'
'What music band?'
'Ray is creating a band called 'Rainbow.' His music will be released globally, and the entire world will listen to his music.' Charu was listening. She saw her daughter is flying with happiness, But the only concern was, would her dad accept this relationship? And what would happen when her dad would come to know this bizarre love story?

Will Jyotika go against her dad's wish?

She was very scared of the thought of the forthcoming thunder.

The story will not end here. The biggest question is Sunny! The boy whom Jyotika never liked as her life partner. They grew together since their childhood. Jyotika grew up and started taking her life's decisions on her own. Children grow and leave their parents, for their friends and love. Their priorities change. They do not want parents to interfere, especially this generation.

All rich houses have the same problem of putting their efforts to turn the house in to 'a home'. They have everything except time and emotions for each other. Charu had done the same thing, over the years. Games kept her fit. Her husband liked to compliment her even today, almost everyday and night.

Jyotika looked at the wardrobe and decided to wear a navy blue top and red skirt. She was ready to leave but mom? . . . She was definitely going to stop her for breakfast and she did.

'You will not go out without having breakfast.' 'Mom I am getting late.'
'No, everything can wait.' Charu is very particular about her health. That's her prerogative. And these are the things in which Indian women seek their happiness.

Charu noticed the glow on her daughter's face, she was wearing black sleeveless and maroon skirt. She was paying attention on her dress, an extra attention. Love, the killing emotion she knew how aggressive it is. She fell in love with Mohit, when she was young and her parents forced her to get married to Pratap Sanyal, a Worli based businessman. Mohit wasn't poor, but her father was very much against choosing Mohit, who just knew painting and nothing else.

'I always portray your paintings.' She was amazed to see her own paintings in different colours. Was it her? She asked herself many times. A still picture couldn't do what the painting had done.

She couldn't sleep that night. Mohit was rich.

'I don't have to do anything else, we have enough for both of us. We will make our home, I will exhibit my paintings all over the world with your help. My dad was in shipping company. He has seen enough sea and water. I do not want to even make a painting of sea or water, I do not use water paint for that matter.' Mohit was adamant. They met in an exhibition and became friends, the friendship turned into love one day, when he portrayed her in his paintings. Dehradun was a small place. The college where his paintings were exhibited for the first time was far from the city. Charu was helping Mohit and she didn't realize it became dark that evening. They were alone as everyone had left. She was far from fear. She was ready to face anyone and any situation for her love Mohit. In the candle light, Mohit was creating a master piece of her painting, she, like an obedient girl obeyed whatever he said, 'Open your long hair spread it on you shoulder from front, and remove your dress.' Mohit came back, unbuttoned her Kurta and she let it happen. Next day, his painting was talk of the town, not only the college but the entire city talked about it. The print media displayed the painting on front page, critics appreciated it, a bold live painting. Dad was furious. 'How dared she? How could she? Who would marry her now?'

Mohit was busy in Delhi, collecting awards for his painting, which had made him a star painter overnight.

She was facing heat in the family.

'We will marry soon.' He made an announcement like a free man who cared for no one but his painting.

'What about our parents?'

'If they agree, fine . . . or else we will marry against their wish.' He hugged, kissed and pronounced decision. He didn't ask what was her wish. He knew that. He always thought of her as his wife.

Charu conveyed her wish and her dad rejected outrightly.

'Never to a man who sold his wife for awards.' Her dad pronounced the decision.

'We will commit suicide,' She tried to threaten.

'Love makes everyone unhappy, it can't make you two happy. Do not think anything like this, your father has spoken to one of our relatives who is a very big match maker. You are getting married soon.' Mother was also a staunch, father's supporter.

She fought with herself for many seconds, minutes, hours and days, and bogged to the marriage decided by her parents, writing a letter to Mohit.

'Sorry, I am not a man and powerful like you all. So I couldn't make it. Going by my parents decision'. The letter reached to him through her friend Kamini. He read the letter and looked at her.

'You didn't deserve to be my wife you are coward.' He replied immediately. Kamini brought the reply letter. The same day my mother announced that, I am getting married to a rich Bombay businessman.

Pratap was a typical husband. Honeymoon, shopping, jewelry and comfort at home and good sex at bed were in his definition of marriage and love. He praised only when she was on bed, his morning began with a kiss, tea, newspapers and business calls. She had to manage everything including his specs. She knew she was pretty. Her painter boyfriend won an award showing her body; what else could be best to measure a beautiful body like her!

Later, she used to listen Mohit's name in media for his painting and award and also a girl's name Anamika as his girlfriend. She was an actress he used to visit Jahangir Art Gallery.

That was Monday, Pratap had left for office already. She was not feeling well. She saw the name of Mohit on the last page of the newspaper.

Famous painter Mohit Rawat committed suicide. Did she kill her, did she? No way. She tried to convince herself. A man called her a cowardly, did a coward act, committed suicide! These men are very weak inside, they pretend the opposite, but that's not the truth. The truth was, she loved him. The another truth was Jyotika is in love with a musician. Only she knew, why Jyotika was mad after him.

When did you last fly?

When did you fly . . .
Drop falling
Rain slowing like slow motion
Emotion was washing away
I saw you flying in rain
Moving out of the running train.
Me,
then asked—
You are moving . . .
Walking . . .
But, tell me . . .
When did you fly last . . .

'Wow awesome! What a thought! Once more please 'Jyotika insisted after listening to the poem. Ray kissed her. She smiled. Ray is wild when he makes love.

'Let's go to your music room.'
'Let me kiss you more.'
'No!'
'Yes!'

She didn't know what to do, she began to look into his eyes. Ray's touch was hasty, sometimes hurting. He didn't wait for her response.

She sometimes thought that Sunny had never done this, never expressed anything like this. May be because of his orthodox ideas about touching a girl without marrying her or, perhaps he was waiting to propose her first and then he might start being more with her. Or, just simply that, he didn't like his girlfriend to be touched at all before reaching to a certain understanding.

Ray would take life too lightly on the other hand. Sunny was too serious about life. For Sunny everything should be planned, but Ray didn't know, what planning means.

They got ready to leave for the music room. Ray's house was full of artifacts. Ray's mom Menka's painting was displayed on the living room wall.

Mom was a painter, son was a poet; the entire atmosphere was different from her house. Jyotika could go on talking with them for hours. They discussed poetry, painting, and music. Ray had amazing collection of songs. They loved watching films together. Their likings were very similar. Menka, Ray's mother, was taking care of this house ever since Ray lost his father. Ray was very young when his father died. He was left with just a home, a 1000 square feet flat in Bandra east. She had to sell all her jewelry to survive. Ray was only five years old, when she decided to work on a freelance job. Robin, one of Ray's father's friends helped her to get freelance accounting job from the bank. The same cooperative bank hired Menka as an employee later. Today she was chief manager. The bank was close to her home. Robin and many of her husband's friends always offered help.

Tushar, her husband, was a very popular person. He was a social man, always ready to help others. She met Tushar, fell in love with him and made a wonderful family. They loved each other. Life was comfortable without having any bank balance. Ray came in their life two years after their marriage.

Jyotika felt lively, full of life in there company, music, poetry, songs, paintings, movies and lots of love. Her time would pass in no time with them.

Jyotika kissed him in front of everyone and he didn't hesitate. He was moody, lazy and would always reach late. She hated this. She remembered he was one hour late in his investor's meeting, Malkani was very angry when Ray reached there.

'You are late.'
'I know sir, traffic . . .'
'I don't like people who are late.'
'You may hate people for anything sir, a piece of advice,' he said with smile. 'I don't like this, you are a professional.'
'I am not, I am a music director trying to help you out.' 'You are trying to help me out?'
'Yes sir.'
'Okay, explain me how?'
'I need a glass of water.' Malkani was upset as he was the one who was going to invest money in his project and Ray was talking as if he was doing a favour on Malkani. He wanted to know this boy, who was dictating terms on him. Malkani sat relaxed looking at him. Ray had a glass of water brought by the peon.

'A good project which will rock the world with original music composition, you should not miss the opportunity to make money and name, that's my sincere advice to you!' Malkani didn't say anything, listening, he thought that this boy was trying to fool him.

'In India there are hardly projects where people work on original composition.'

'I am not interested.' The moment Ray heard that, he was out from the office without wasting a second. He didn't forget to smile while he was leaving.

'What happened?' Next day, the entire music team wanted to know. Excited to hear the good news.

'We have to practice the music for some more time having no dead line, that's the way we can create a piece of class.' Ray announced with smile.

Next day, everyone began practice without any hitch. His friends listened to him and trusted him completely. Jyotika liked his team. Joy, Bosky, Manoj Jain, Rehman, Shubh, Vandy . . . A team of seven music players, a rainbow. Joy and Bosky are blind. Both were amazing guitarists and singers too. Manoj Jain helped Ray in composing, programming music, Shubh was a drummer. What a team! She was fascinated. This kind of a team only Ray can create! Bosky loved music, her world was music. Joy wanted to see the world, he wanted light, brightness. He hated his handicapped eyes, but Bosky was okay with it. She had no issue with it. She could hear and feel the music that was enough for her. Joy's questions were full of curiosity. 'How does Ray's girlfriend look like?' Joy asked one day in the music room.

'She is a bomb man!'

'What do you mean? Explain to me man.

'Joy smiled and asked. She has sexy thighs big boobs, sensuous lips and . . . And? . . . he thought what to say . . . 'And . . .' Joy was interested to know.

'She is very soft . . . her skin is delicate and soft like butter you know how butter feels when you touch.'

'Ya, but how do you know, have you touched and felt her too?'

'Ya, he touched me many times. He slept with me many times Joy, you also wan'na sleep?' Both Shubh and Joy didn't notice that, Jyotika was standing right behind them listening to them, they couldn't notice her. Both of them were frozen. Jyotika was very angry.

'You guys have only sex and filth in mind and do not know how to talk in a decent way.'

'I am sorry.' Joy began to repent.

'Come on yaar chill why are you so angry, I was praising you.'

'In his own way!' Bosky joined them. He must be talking nasty? I know Shubh, he talks about me too.'

'What happened?' Ray joined them who was outside of the music room with Vandy and Rehman.

'They are having crush on your girlfriend'. Bosky informed.

'Really? If so, be it.'

'Yes, both of them like me.' Jyotika got involved in conversation and started enjoying the fun talking.

'Joy sings like an ass and Shubh plays like horse and both of them are trying to hit my girlfriend, no one on this earth can snatch her from me you dolts.'

Though Ray joked, but Jyotika smelt jealousy, which Ray never showed. It wasn't just a light joke, some concern was there too. Jyotika loved watching Ray being jealous and concerned.

It was fun to be with Ray and his team. Manoj and Rehman both loved Vandy. They kept on fighting over Vandy. Vandy had dusky complexion. She was tall and very attractive. She really had a great voice.

7

Sunny was planning Jyotika's birthday as an opportunity to mark on impact and impress everyone.

Charu was really scared this time on Jyotika's birthday. It was a very big event as her husband always had organized a lavish party and he personally remained involved in it and saw that everyone should come to his daughter's birthday party. After all, all his hard work was for her only! She had apprehensions, she didn't know what? But she had an intuition that something wrong was going to happen. She knew her husband, he would never accept Jyotika's new friends on her birthday.

But, something different happened that day! Everyone came for the birthday party, all his friends, relatives, business professionals, traders except Jyotika and his friends. The birthday girl was absconding from the big event, celebrating her birthday with her musical team.

Sunny was surprised it wasn't expected. He planned to give her a diamond necklace, an expensive one. The guests were asking and were waiting for Jyotika, her father was unable to answer them, where her daughter was; and why she was not attending her own birthday. Sunny decided not to wait for her, he left early to meet a very important client. He thought if Jyotika was not there he might utilize the time.

Jyotika came very late. Lights of the corridor and living room were turned on again, when she came. Her father was worried but he kept quiet, thinking that it was not the right time to ask where she was for the whole evening. 'You must be very tired Jyotika?'

'Ya, I am,' Jyotika said and left for her room to have a shower.

Both of them didn't speak for a while. Charu didn't know what to say since everything was so obvious. She knew everything. She had all the answers, so there was no point in fooling themselves by asking questions. She had chosen to be somewhere, with someone but her parents. And her parents didn't understand what to say and how to say.

Charu opened the gift box brought by Sunny, a diamond necklace! She showed it to Jyotika when she came from shower. She was called by Charu to see these gifts especially Sunny's gift.

She smiled. She knew, Sunny brings gifts like this. He was a person, any girl would love to be with! But Ray was incomparable. He was unique, a genius. Ray's smile was her gift. Yes, that smile was her life time gift. She was with them and everyone brought something, even Joy brought a flute, but Ray didn't bring anything, Ray's mom brought a yellow Suit, a skirt and top.

Jyotika took the necklace and went inside her room. She threw the necklace box in the jewelry drawer of her cupboard. Her father was silent. He couldn't scold her. He never had. But he had right to be angry with her and he was. He would not talk to Jyotika for sometime if he was angry. All the conversations began through her mother till the time they arrived at compromise and sort out the problem.

Jyotika knew that there was no point in discussing the issue. She went inside the room, had shower and went to bed. Charu entered.

'We will talk tomorrow' Jyotika said in a dictating voice.

'Baby, your dad is upset, and he has a valid reason for that, and I also feel that he is very right. You shouldn't have spent your birthday with someone else, while everyone was waiting here for you!' Charu was upset too.

'We will talk later mamma. What's wrong. I told you. I am really tired, please.' Jyotika was little aggressive. Charu moved out from Jyotika's room thinking, may be it was not the right time to talk to her.

It was a very big decision of Jyotika not to remain present at her own birthday party. She didn't even consider that it might result into some serious effects. She didn't even want to discuss about it!

Sunny was driving alone after finishing his meeting. He was really disturbed. He didn't want to meet Jyotika any more. He knew he had failed in love. He was not ready to accept his defeat, and who was against him? An unsuccessful, unemployed person like Ray! A music freak!

Koyal! He wanted to see Koyal. He turned his car and drove to the place where he can find Koyal. 1:00 O'clock! He saw the watch. Koyal had business sense and she always had made right decision. Sunny had supported her decisions always, even though sometimes he knew that, her decision might cause the loss, but still he had supported Koyal, even though it was risky. He had taken risks to win and he had won; always! He called her and told her that he was coming. He knew that she was normally awake late night, she had a habit of reading books till late.
'This time? Is everything alright?' Koyal was surprised.
'Yes, just I thought to have a cup of coffee with you.'
'Come on in, the coffee is waiting.' Koyal was happy for he was coming. He was always welcomed in her life. She knew where she was heading . . . a dead end. This guy was not going to spend his life with her. He was in love with Jyotika. But it didn't make any difference to her. She was ready to suffer for a great guy like Sunny.

Koyal was a model. She left modeling and joined his company. They had been working hard to develop a company like this. She, loved Sunny, that was the only important thing for her. She hoped that one day Sunny, her love, might come back to her. For Sunny she had sacrificed her modeling career. Not only this, she was also ready to sacrifice her life for Sunny. She was mad for him, any how she wanted Sunny's company. And even if he would have married to Jyotika, she would have his company in the office. Finally, love is nothing but having company of your loved ones. No one could have snatched him from her.

She opened the door. Hugged him and smiled looking at Sunny. Sunny was sad. He tried to smile back. She knew Sunny and his smiles.

'So?'

'So?'

'Your turn Sweetie, I asked first!' Koyal said frankly. Sunny smiled again.

'It doesn't matter at all to me who said what.' 'So how was the birthday party? Did she like the necklace?' Sunny didn't say anything.

'You look upset?'

'Yes . . . I am.'

'What can I do for you Sunny?'

'Coffee! A cup of coffee is fine.' Koyal's house had a huge open balcony. They sat there with a cup of coffee. She was wearing shorts and spaghetti. She was looking very sexy. It was a full moon night and the moon light was touching her legs and arms. Anyone would have gone mad touching her. Both of them were there, looking at the sky, lost in their own thoughts. Sunny loved that moment. Koyal knew silence has meaning more than words.

The road down at the distance looked far off from the balcony, the street light was trying to make it visible as much as it can. Sunny looked at the road. Where did he go wrong? What did he do? A life without Jyotika was unthinkable? What should he do and how should he make things fall in place? The shadow of the street light shook vehemently when the cars' light hit it.

8

*M*orning, 8 am

'What is going on in this house? Someone please tell me.' Pratap was angry. 'This is not your office! Do not pretend as if you are talking to your personal secretary. This is your home and you should know what's going on! Don't ask me again and again and also let me clarify one thing, if you talk like this, then you won't be able to handle Jyotika's situation. She has grown up taking her own decisions independently.' Charu made her point of view with warning attached to it.

'She is a very emotional girl, and if she gets hurt, I do not know what step she will take. She may leave this house. We need to understand her with calm mind'.

Charu didn't want any heated discussion and fight in the house, the servants would gossip about it outside, she knew how rumors are spread.

'She will never do that. I know her.' Pratap advocated.

'I am telling you sweetheart, she is in love with this guy and if you want Jyotika to listen to you, talk very calmly.'

'Where is she?' Pratap said in low voice.

'Sleeping.'

'Hmm! What should I do then, budge to whatever she wants and spoil her life? He is a music director. What would I tell my friends, relatives . . . That my son-in-law is good for nothing, a musical who is a loser and plays guitar and drum, and my daughter is in love with this idiot?'

'You can think about it! Sort it out, talk with Jyotika, but let me warn you, I am not here to clean your mess this time, I am not your mediator in this matter.' Charu threatened.

'Have you lost it? What's wrong with you?'

'Nothing, just telling you, enough is enough!'

'Call this guy; meet him. May be this kind of positive approach and conversation will make Jyotika to be on our side and analyze the situation meanwhile! Sunny has his own personality impact too, she treats him as friend. These things are temporary. She has fallen in love with a boy who has no background. She actually loves music, not Ray. Try and understand that. She is having fun out there.' Charu explained the situation in broad light. This man is good for nothing, ready to spoil peace of this house.

'Yes. She is right she might not be getting space with Sunny. He is different. Charu has a point. Aggressive approach will spoil the entire situation. He can't force Jyotika as there is a risk of losing her. Now a days it's happening all over. He has been listening to stories like that,' Pratap Sanyal was reconsidering Charu's suggestion.

'Ok so what am I supposed to do?' Pratap surrendered. Charu knew that. Mostly she listened to her daughter and husband, but at times she used to call the shots and they had to listen to her and follow that when she was tough.

'Call this guy, meet him informally and let's see what he has to say. Do not go against them. Motivate Jyotika that it's her life and she should choose the right guy, we are with her.' The very next day Ray was called.

'My dad wants to meet you.' Jyotika conveyed with smile. 'What for?' Ray pretended.

'To play football!'

'Good idea, at your home?'

'Inside the kitchen.'

'Hmm'

'Hmm'

'Wear formals. Be in time. My dad is very punctual and organized, he doesn't like people who are shabbily dressed.' Jyotika was trying to be as specific as she could. Ray decided to obey. He chose to wear white shirt full sleeves, black cotton trouser and black shoes. He shaved before taking bath. He tried his level best but he was late by 10 minutes.

Jyotika's dad was waiting for Ray. He shook hands with him as he reached Jyotika's home. He didn't forget to hug Jyotika tight. Her parents noticed that. Fair, straightforward, smart, confident and creative music director, small family of only a mother and son; not a bad deal! Pratap thought for a second. But Sunny? Sunny can't be compared with him. No comparison for a nationally reputed brand owner.

Pratap was surprised to see his confidence. He felt he is facing someone who is not very easy to handle.

'Pleasure meeting you . . .' Pratap pretended not remembering his name and as if he was not that important.

'Ray, his name is Ray papa,' Jyotika replied.

'Ray, what do you do? I have heard that you play music.'

'I compose music, I am a lyricist and poet. But you can call me a music director, I will not mind' he smiled. 'And how many compositions have you made, Mr. Music director?' He was being sarcastic, trying to demoralize Ray.

'Many, do you want me to sing one of them?'

'No . . . no just asking.'

'And you make money also?'

'Definitely, you see,' he took a pause, breathed in silence for a while, shook his body, looked at Charu and Jyotika and replied back.' Music is a very profitable business, globally, you should also try this, besides making money, you will become famous too sir. People know you through your music. Let me assure you, you will be known as Ray's father in law.' Pratap ignored his statement he knew he was trying to be smart.

'Hmm! You do not seem to be comfortable?'

'I am not used to these clothes.'

'Why?'

'Tight! These are fit, usually I wear loose trousers and shirts.'

'So why are you wearing these clothes then.' Pratap smiled. 'I have to respect my love's decision sometimes.' Ray smiled this time.

Silence for a moment.

No one was talking . . . Charu smiled looking at him. Cute boy! She had no problem with him at all. Ray was like Mohit, the only difference was Mohit was silent many a times, Ray had great energy and great sense of humor. Ya she was her daughter and would fall in love with an artiste, which she did. She knew her daughter would choose someone like him only. Sunny and he couldn't be compared because they were completely different from each other.

'What would you like to have?' Charu broke the silence.

'Proper lunch, I am hungry.' Pratap smiled when Ray looked at him.

Charu left to see that things should be organized according to the special guest.

'Jyotika bring me my ring, it's in my bedroom drawer' Jyotika was surprised why suddenly dad wanted his ring. She ignored him for a moment, she wanted to pay attention to the conversation happening between him and Ray.

'I feel very awkward when I don't wear my ring. Can you bring that ring?' Jyotika smiled unwillingly and left, meanwhile Pratap got a chance to talk important points he thought to discuss with Ray which might have made Ray change his decision and not to indulge in marriage with Jyotika.

'Jyotika is my only daughter, so anybody who gets married to Jyotika will have to stay in this house as our son-in-law. I hope you are aware of this fact.'

'I wasn't sir, but I am now. I have no problem at all! You have a big house, me and my mom can stay here. Do you have any problem if my mother stays with me in this house, sir? Ray was sharp and smart in his answers, he replied quickly, without a second thought and that was the worry for Pratap. Meanwhile, Jyotika arrived saying that she couldn't find any ring in his drawer.

'I did not find any ring there, sorry.'

'It's ok if you can't find it' Pratap said releasing a long breath.

Ray was very vocal during lunch, he was relishing food, appreciating it, being friendly with servants, talking to Jyotika's mom, laughing, cracking jokes, the entire house atmosphere was changed. Jyotika was very happy seeing him mixing with her family members. But Pratap was not happy, he didn't know what to do with this guy who was so smart, making everyone friendly! And no way he wanted to lose Sunny, who was cool and calm and busy building a property worth millions by working day and night. Also, what was he going to say to his relatives, friends, professional friends? Was he going to say that his son-in-law is a music director, a singer, an orphan, who has no background? How insulting! But he could not do anything then, he had to say yes to the marriage. The conversation between Pratap and Charu concluded discussing how Sunny will react to this marriage. Jyotika was confident.

'Sunny is my best friend and I will make him understand everything.'

Sunny was discussing with Koyal about the appointments of new people in the company, meanwhile he got a call from Jyotika,

'Hi Jyotika, how are you?. No, I am free, tell me . . . I have absolutely no problem, ok, evening 8 O' clock.'

9

The beautiful lights of the restaurant had made the evening glorious, having elegant crowd, ladies with designer dresses to compliment the atmosphere, having chin up, with arrogance, which meant, I am the beautiful here with rich man accompanying me!

Sunny was alone, waiting for Jyotika.

Jyotika as usual came late, Sunny was in time. She took no time to announce the purpose of the meeting. Before Sunny could understand anything, she started, 'You are my best friend Sunny but Ray is the love of my life. I want to get married to him. He came to meet my dad today.' Sunny was zapped. He couldn't believe that he was hearing this. It was very difficult for Sunny to believe this news. Sunny said, 'I accept and welcome your decision, we are still friends, would you like to have something?' He was still trying to be nice with Jyotika, in spite of feeling hurd from inside. The meeting ended with fresh lime soda which both of them shared.

10

Sunny was out that night. He asked his driver to go home with the car. He switched off his cell-phone and took a taxi. He wanted to be alone. Everything had become meaningless for him . . .

He felt completely devastated. He was not knowing, where will he go from there. He was proved to be a loser for the first time in life! He suddenly realized that all his hard work, planning, complete focus on work had no meaning at all! Everything cannot be transformed into positive results, especially love and personal sentiments and emotions. One can't impress someone by his achievements, destiny too has a role to play in life.

'As you can't change your past, same applies with your future. That is what destiny is,' his mom said once, when he was very young.

'Future and past can't be changed.' He still remembered his mom's face, she had broad forehead and long neck.

Whitish, cute looking, soothing, mind blowing smile she had! Whenever he was down, sad, depressed he missed his mom. His father too never thought of any woman after his mom expired. 'She was very kind, passionate and cool lady, full of positive energy'. His father mentioned many times thinking of her wife. He had seen his father seeing her photograph every morning and night.

He saw that the sand could shine only when it met the moon light. After almost three hours of silence, he decided to switch on the phone.

There were so many missed call alerts! Calls from his father, Koyal and many more calls. He called up his father and assured that he would be back soon, he wanted to be alone for sometime. While, he was talking to his dad he found that Koyal was calling on the second line, he spoke to Koyal next.

'Your dad was worried and he was calling me every 10-12 minutes, where are you?' Koyal was curious to know.
'I am fine, at Chowpati, where are you?'
'I am at home.'
'Do you want me to come to Chowpatty beach?'
'Okay . . .' Sunny's reply was short. He started walking on the sand thinking how this happened in his life. Koyal came fast, She took half an hour to reach there. Both of them were quiet for sometime.
'I heard from your dad, I am sorry about it.' Koyal was sympathetic. Have you had dinner?'

Both of them went for dinner in a restaurant. Silence, they had nothing to discuss between them. Sunny was looking at her, Koyal was wearing pink sleeveless top and black skirt. She was so pretty that she looked beautiful in all her dresses.
'You are not eating anything.'

Koyal noticed that Sunny was not having anything. Sunny had no answer, he was silent. Thinking nothing . . .blank, didn't know what to think and remember! Things had gone worst. Jyotika had come to him and said "no". She didn't love him, she loved a music director. A music director? What rubbish! What music? Who is he? What has he done? n innocent idiot girl! She hasn't seen the world, I know she will spoil everything she has!' Sunny couldn't stop the chain of thoughts, straining his mind. 'Best friend my foot! I am her best friend! Why should I be a best friend of someone, who doesn't care for me?'

Occupied and frustrated with these thoughts he wanted fresh air. Wanted to divert his mind's attention but was not able to. This would take some time . . . he knew.

Both of them were ready to leave. Sunny had hardly touched anything, Koyal knew he would not. Koyal paid the bill, smiled looking at him. Both began to walk down the stairs. Both knew they are fully occupied with thoughts. Koyal knew that few steps ahead they had to decide who would go where? Would they be spending some more time together? They were standing outside the hotel lobby.

'Where is your car?' Koyal looked at him. He was blank.

'Ya,. Where is my car?' He tried to remember.

'You must have left at the beach side.' Koyal wanted to reassure it. He didn't reply. 'I will call your driver to find out.' Koyal made a call and came to know that Sunny had actually come by taxi.

'Poor guy, out of his mind! He is such a hardworking, sincere guy and now he is traveling in a taxi.'

Koyal took him to her house. She knew he can't be left alone. Sunny was lost in his thoughts.

She went to change her clothes. Sunny sat in the living room. He walked to the balcony to breathe some fresh air. Koyal joined him very soon, wearing shorts and spaghetti.

In the morning, at around 10 O'clock Sunny got up. He slept with Koyal in her flat. He tried to remember about what had happened, but he had a headache. Last night . . . nightmare? No it actually happened! Jyotika was no more with him and he came with Koyal in her flat. He was resting, thinking and then . . . Yes, both of them came to the bed room. She was trying to make him sleep. She touched his forehead. It was relaxing. She hugged him tight and . . . he was in deep sleep. But where was Koyal?

'Good morning!' Koyal entered having coffee in her hand, smiling.

'Good morning, papa might be worried . . .'

'I called him in the morning that you are here.' He was worried actually, I made him understand and told him not to worry I am taking care of you.' He smiled looking at her.

'Thank you, Koyal' he got up and hugged her.

'I do not want to go to office today, I am going home,' Sunny said. Sunny saw the marble floor was cleaned well. The bed is right at the middle and the furniture has been changed.

'You have got new furniture?'

'Ya, only in the bed room'. Koyal replied having the coffee sipped.

The window was opening and shutting down as fast wind was forcing it to do so. Koyal got up to shut the window. Sunny noticed tall fair sexy legs. She came back sat down showing her cleavage.

'You have bath. A good bath would help you to relax.' Koyal offered.

'Not a bad idea'.

'I called a shop close by, just besides the society gate. I have asked him to bring new pyjama Kurta of free size. It would fit to you.'

Inside the bathroom there was a big white bath tub. Koyal helped him to sink in the warm water. She helped him to bath and be in the water for longer time.

The call bell rang and she went to open the door. She took the dress. She came back in the bathroom, Sunny was laying down in the water closing his eyes.

Koyal helped him with soap rubbing on his shoulder. Sunny was in the bathroom almost for 45 minutes. He came out with a good feeling, stress had erased.

Sunny went inside the bathroom, changed the dress available there, a white Kutra Pyjama.

11

*J*yotika got up late around 12:30 pm.

She slept very late. Last night she was with Ray and the group, playing music, celebrating. The music played loud and everyone danced.

She was very happy. Joy sang and Bosky accompanied him. She was very tired.

She felt a high, Ray being hers, last night. Everything was amazing.

Her phone was switched off. She switched it on. There were sms alerts of missed calls from Menka, Vandy, Rehman, Manoj. She got a call from Manoj as she switched her phone on. 'Come to the hospital asap.' His voice was shattering.

'What's wrong?'

'You please come as soon as possible'. Something has gone wrong horribly.

She thought while getting ready. Charu looked at her with silent eyes and didn't utter a single word. She didn't ask her to have breakfast.

She let her go.

'Why mom was looking at me like this?' She asked herself. The driver was waiting for her to take her to somewhere. Her phone was ringing continuously. Everyone, almost everyone called including Menka with the same answer,

'Come asap.'

'Who is not well? What went wrong? Everyone called except one RAY . . .! Ray didn't call. He doesn't have cell may be? But he calls in a situation like this, where everyone is concerned, Ray would have called for sure. He normally has Menka aunt's cell. Why then he didn't speak to her? Is he sick? But last night he was okay. Exertion may be?' She convinced herself.

She was restless inside the car, looking at the road.

'Ronak Singh drive fast,' she said being restless. She entered the hospital. Manoj and Vandy were waiting for her.

'What happened?' Jyotika asked.

'Ray has met with an accident,' Vendy said and they moved inside.

'How is he now?' Jyotika asked.

No one spoke, they moved inside. Something is terribly wrong as she rightly had apprehensions.

'*Ray has met an accident,*' Vandy's voice over resounded.

Menka was crying, Joy, Bosky, Rehman, Shubh everyone was standing and crying.

Menka hugged her with tears in eyes.

'Why? What happened? Is Ray not ok? Where is he? May be in operation theatre,' she was thinking.

'*Ray has left us. He is no more.*' Someone said. The words pronounced, vibrated in the trans, her mind went in dark.

'What she hearing is the truth or . . .Yes, it is!'

Ray is dead. That's the reason everyone is in the hospital. She made herself believe.

'A truck hit him at around 10:15 am in the morning. He had left home for going to music room,' Rehman informed the police inspector.

'How did he reach here?'

'Manish and his friends, they are college students they took him in taxi and brought here'.

Inspector Naina took the statement. Jyotika overheard the conversation. She was standing quietly with Menka. Ray is dead. Ray of her life had repressed.

Dr. Anand approached them. He took Menka inside the cabin. She watched both of them through the glass. Dr. Anand was saying something, trying to convince some point, it seemed.

Charu came and brought her home. Charu tried to console. 'People leave people. We have to honor God's wish'.

Jyotika didn't utter a word. She kept looking outside the window.

She slept whole day, Menka gave her sleeping pill on doctor's advice. Pratap asked about her many times as how is she feeling. Sunny visited her.
'I am sorry.' Sunny was sad. Charu hinted Sunny, not to talk about Ray's death as Jyotika would again feel sad. She came to know that Ray's eyes have been given to Joy and Bosky. Dr. Anand did the operation, who knew Ray very well.

Jyotika was not aware about the fact that, Both eyes go to two people, one each. Everything became normal, except her state of mind. It was hard to believe that, Ray was no more. She used to go to Ray's house and used to sit quietly in his room where both of them spent lot of times together.

Inspector Naina Muke visited the accident venue.
The truck hit the footpath, Ray might be walking on that. He hit against a tree when truck hit him.
'It's a simple accident case.' Her assistant Rawat informed with conclusion, to shut the file. The driver got bail and went home.

Something was wrong, Inspector Naina smelt a rat. The brake failed, it was possible, but how come he went to the footpath. She visited the place and the truck. She found one empty envelope. The envelope had a name which had been tried to be erased. She sent the envelope to forensic lab. She was known as a capable police inspector.

She knew accidents were smart tools to murder some one. Who wanted to kill Ray and why? Did someone conspire the killing? Had someone contracted to kill him in accident? Evidence hinted 'may be'. The truck had gone suddenly from footpath to the road. The truck was moving in the right direction, it's brake failed as claimed by the truck driver but how come the straight moving truck moved in different direction. Inspector wanted to go deep till the core of the case.

'I want all his friends', relatives' background, and recently has something happened unpleasant?' She told her assistant Rawat to find out Rawat had great respect for his boss Naina. He had never worked with such a sincere officer and he was always proud of her. Rawat didn't have to struggle hard to find out.

'A team of seven, of which Joy and Bosky are blind, Shubh is drummer, Manoj is Ray's assistant, Vandy, Rehman are singers. Ray was the seventh and the team leader. Simple guys having tough time to dream their future without Ray'. Rawat reported back to Naina.

'What about Sunny? Sunny's family? This girl Jyotika, her parents? Have you got their details too, go find that too.' Rawat was put on the job again.

Rawat began his investigations again.

12

*S*unny arrived at Jyotika's place after two days, Jyotika was withered, sad and down. Sunny left his office to be with her. 'Life is like that! You are never sure of anything! Anything can happen anytime, that's what life is, we cannot do anything . . .' Jyotika appreciated his presence.

Sunny did everything to bring back a smile on her face. Jyotika's parents felt obliged whenever Sunny was at home. They were always very receptive towards Sunny.

The very next day of the accident Jyotika was with Menka. She had convinced herself that Ray had gone somewhere in the dark and not going to come back in the light again! She started looking at his stuff. Each and every corner of the house had some memory left about the time they have spent together. Jyotika got an old diary of Ray in which he had written his poetry. She started reading one of them.

ONE

Me not me;
You are not you;
There is a vacuum only.
Space remains . . .
In that space,
Everyone is no One;
Everyone is in that One.
We search that One -
Where there is no One;
Where there is no One.

13

*J*oy opened his eyes after the operation, with slight anxiety and a bit of fear.

He was wearing dark glasses.

He looked at the window, the hospital room. He could see some glossy light entering inside the room. The door, the wall, the window and the nurse. Human activities, hand movements, mouth and lips move when someone says something. This act is different from smell and touch. He touched the wall to feel. The nurse smiled and helped him to see outside the window. He looked at the garden and grass and many people walking. A man walking with a stick in his hand.

'What is that?'
'A man is walking.'
'What is that thing?'
'He is walking with a stick.' Joy focused at the stick. 'What's your name sister?'
'Mary John.'
'What is that, hanging on the wall?'
'A calendar.' Yes! He had heard people talking about it many times. He saw his reflection on the window glass, which was closed ajar.
'Can I see myself?'

'Yes! You can look there.' Joy saw a face with dark eyeglasses. His face! It was not very clear. He tried to remove the glare.

'Do not do that, you have to use it for sometime.' Mary John objected politely.

'Till when?' 'Dr. R. K. Anand would explain it better.' Joy raised his left hand to see whether it's his reflection in the window glass? Was it the same or not? It was. It smiled when he smiled. He was convinced then. He then became sure that, it was him. Mary smiled looking at him. She knew, it happens when a blind gets vision.

'How do I look?' Joy asked.

'What do you mean?'

'Am I good . . . good looking? Sister?'

'Yes, you are.'

'How? Can you explain it to me?'

'I can try. You are cute, you have dimples on your cheeks, when you smile, you are fair.' Joy tried to smile and saw his dimples on his cheeks in the window glass.

'Hmm . . .Thanks! These are the only measures to say, if someone is handsome or beautiful?' He smiled.

'It is very complicated. It is many a times a matter of personal choice also.' Mary tried to summarize the conversation. She was used to replying all these questions. Joy observed a white long bar fixed on the wall. 'What's that?'

'A tube light.' Mary replied. Joy was offered a glass of water. He took it, saw the glass.

'What's the color of the glass?'

'Its off white, you can say?' She wasn't sure.

'And what's the color of the water? Do you know that?' Mary saw the water and thought for a while.

'Water color! It's called water color. It wears any color you mix in it.'

Menka entered the room. Joy looked at her.

'Do you recognize me? I am your doctor.'

'I know who you are Menka aunty, your fragrance is enough for me to guess this.' Joy said with confidence.

'How do you feel?'

'Pleasantly surprised after having a new life!' Joy looked at Menka aunty.

'Is she beautiful too? Is she fair? Has she dimples too?' He started observing her. Tried to notice if she gets dimple while smiling.

Is she also a good looking lady if she has dimples? What is the parameter for deciding if the looks of a person are good looking or not? Fair, cute? Is she cute?

'I will come in a minute, I have to see Bosky.' Menka said and left. 'Is she beautiful too?' Joy asks.

'She is very pretty.' Mary replied with a smile.

'Can you explain?'

'Have patience, you would know.'

'How does Bosky look like?' He started thinking.

'Is she good looking also? And what about Jyotika? Yes! There were talks in the music room, she is very pretty.'

Menka came back.

'Bosky is still sleeping.' Menka said and took an apple and knife. She cut the apple into pieces. Joy was watching her hands and finger movements. For him everything seemed so interesting.

He took the knife to hold it. He looked at it. Smiled. Menka took the knife and kept it back in the basket. She knew, for him it's a new object. He kept on observing things, comparing Menka's face with Mary, looking outside the window, looking at himself in the mirror again and again.

The tube light was switched on. He had heard about it. 'Electricity! Because of electricity this tube light burns and spreads light in the room; and because of that, everyone who has vision can see.' He knew, only eyes are not enough. One needs appropriate light, tube light, bulb light, candle light or any artificial light other than sunlight to see the object.

Joy fell asleep after sometime.

Menka went home after assuring that, Joy and Bosky were fine. Joy's mind was seeing images with stories, mixed with thoughts getting converted into incidents. Menka, nurse, mirror, garden sunlight, tube light.

His dreams were never like these, there were hazy images. Those images now took some shapes and actuated with a little clarity, when he was in deep sleep.

He saw an imaginary girl talking to him. Her face was not clear, he was trying to make out who she was? Jyotika or Bosky? He was trying to touch, smell and feel the same way he had done many times before, to identify a person. The girl was saying something, he heard his name.

'Joy' . . . Joy are you listening?' He opened his eyes suddenly, to find a girl actually talking to him.

He got up and sat on the bed facing that girl. She was smiling.

He breathed in a familiar smell. Jyotika! He looked at her. A girl was staring at him, sitting on a chair besides his bed.

'I was instructed not to disturb you, but couldn't stop myself from waking you.' Jyotika was as commanding as she was always.

She is really beautiful. Joy didn't feel the need to ask anyone. He had understood by now that, beauty attracts you. Her face was oval, sharp nose, fascinating lips, her skin, pounding out of the sleeveless dress was shining. She was graceful, her cleavage was provocative, inviting a person to stare and to see more. She had a perfect figure may be. He found himself staring at her, while she was looking into his eyes.

'I can't imagine you can see through Ray's eyes. It is impossible, made possible, isn't it?'

Jyotika's voice echoed. Her lips moved with vibrations and words pronounced, his ears heard the words matching with what she said. It was such an amazing experience to watch someone speaking, matching the same thought and meaning what the person is trying to say. That didn't happen when the nurse and Menka aunty were speaking. May be he ignored because he wanted to see himself.

'I am asking something Joy!'

'The lips move, ears catch, mind informs to understand. This is how it works.' Joy made himself understand.

'Did you ask something?' He missed the earlier question she asked.

'How do you feel when you see?'

'Adventurous!'

'Ray has contributed to this adventure.'

'Ya, how can I forget that. He was a lifeline for all of us, for our music. He has given a new lease of life to me.' Joy spent about two weeks in the hospital. He was taken home after that. He was sitting with Bosky, on the back seat. Menka was sitting on the front seat with Jyotika, who was driving. He saw Bosky. Her skin color was different from Jyotika. He tried to recall that color, dusky! He could understand colors a bit.

'They are not only seven as claimed to be in the rainbow. There are many more than seven. White, off white, red, maroon, dark red, blood color, sky blue, blue, navy blue, black, yellow, pink, whitish, fair, milky white, grey, dusky, golden, silver; and water color, which cannot be defined. It's just the color of water!'

He observed that, eyes have limitations. They can't see air, particles in air, deep through water. They can see across the transparent glass but can't see across concrete walls. Feelings and emotions can't be seen through eyes. They can be perceived and instilled.

He was struggling to understand all this, ever since he has got vision. He found it an uneasy task. His mind was in a hotchpotch state.

'It will take some time, don't worry'. Jyotika consoled him, when he asked all these questions, while in hospital.

He looked out of the window; the concrete roads were silhouetted by colorful tall buildings, people driving different vehicles of different shapes, speeding on roads.
Bosky was silent, busy looking out on the road.

'Is she beautiful? She is sexy though. He thought . . .long legs, busty figure, graceful face, long hair, she is not fair like Menka and Jyotika but she is good looking. Vision has discovered many new things, the shape and size of the body. The sharp nose and big eyes are features of good looks. A girl with big breast with dusky skin can be called sexy.

He now knew that why someone is called sexy and not beautiful. He remembered the conversations of his friends in the music room.

Joy saw the entire house, Ray's room, his guitar, key board, drum, piano, table, harmonium, everything. He touched and felt the touch. Ray's photograph on the wall. He was smiling, tears rolled out of Joy's and Bosky's eyes.

'You will stay in Ray's room.' Menka had made arrangements beforehand. Everything was decided. For Menka, both were very close, they had her son's eyes.

'And . . . what about me? Where will I sleep?' 'You will stay in my room.'

Menka hugged Bosky with love. Joy for a moment scared being in Ray's room. Ray was a genius. Everyone became nostalgic thinking of Ray.

'I am making tea, who wants to sip a cup of tea?' Menka asked.

'Show me the sunrise and sunset please,' he requested Jyotika, looking at the spoon. This spoon was different from the one which he had seen in the hospital. This was bigger in size and shape.

Jyotika honored his request next morning. The sun was rising in round shape, with reddish rays. The darkness was erasing slowly. Joy was thrilled. The beach was silent early in the morning, quiet and tranquil.

The same day he witnessed the sunset also.

'Magic!' Joy exclaimed.

'This magic appears everyday. No one has time to see this magic.' Joy didn't utter a word, he enjoyed watching the setting sun.

'Hardly few people understand the power of nature; they run after petty happiness and ignore the bigger one.' Joy commented walking on sand.

'See the soil, sand and rock, each is different from the other. There is so much to know. Nature is beautiful, really!'

They walked and stayed on the beach till darkness gripped over.

Joy wanted to explore more about the natural power and beauty.

Joy felt that vision had given him an additional sense to see, know and recognize things. Was he losing the power to smell and touch without vision? Was he? He tried to judge and introspect many times.

Next day, Jyotika took him to Lonavala to show nature. Jyotika drove and took him to the spot which was two thousand feet high from the sea level, on the hills. He was thrilled to see the hills and the height.

It was pouring, weather was cold, they were inside the car. Jyotika came out in the rain. Her T shirt and long skirt drenched in a minute. She dragged Joy out of the car.

'Come on, enjoy the rain.'

'It's chilling! We both might get cold and fever after that, take my words.'

'Let it be, who is scared of that, let's enjoy the rain'.

They got wet in the rain, watching hills from the height, and waterfalls too. They were holding each other's hands for support. Joy felt Jyotika's touch. He was thrilled.

There was a small shade on the height, where corn, tea and onion fritters were being sold. Joy and Jyotika, both were hungry. They decided to walk down to the tin shed. They had corn and tea, sitting under the tin shed, looking at each other. Joy saw young couples were enjoying, hugging tight, kissing each other.

'Ray showed me this place.'

'Was it raining at that time too?'

'Ya.' Jyotika loved talking about those moments.

They enjoyed being there for hours, chatting. Jyotika shared the moments she spent with Ray on Tiger Hills.

For Bosky, these things did not matter at all.

'The mirror tells the color of the skin, shape of the body and marks etc. Does that really make any difference?' She had good height, sexy figure, she could figure out, she looked dashing and killing, smart in jeans and top, her body is little chubby and some extra fat which was fine to make her look sexy.

She observed, Joy was good looking, fair, pleasant, cute. She was happy she had made a good choice, when she even couldn't see his color of skin and beauty measures. Joy had dreamt many times that, one day he will see the world he lives in. The dream had come true. He had only imagined this world. The looks of people, the heights of buildings. He loved observing the material beauty, tree, river, sea, sand, silver, gold, valley, lake, stones, rocks, hills, villages, small town, big town, cities, metro, metropolitan culture, food and costumes, different lifestyles adopted by different people; everything was visible now.

Jyotika loved to make Joy aware about his new world.

'What's that?'
'Trees have different kinds, this is one of them, we call it Pipal. It grows with solid hard branches, so much so that these branches grow downward and enter in the soil.'
'Ya, it looks gigantic.'
'It has long life, may be more than thousand years!'
'Are you sure? To the best of my knowledge, it is a few hundreds and not thousands?'

Jyotika knew that. She answered many queries thrawn by Joy, many of them were sheer guesswork, just to reply because she loved to be with him, to see Ray's one eye, feeling that he is back with the blessing of vision and science. She didn't want to think about why she loved Joy's company? Was it because of Ray's eye or something else? It was interesting to show and help him knowing the world. He was blind who had got vision and want to see things. For him everything was new, like for a kid . . . He stared at her face and body. He examined her throughout, asked stupid questions about her dresses.

'Girls wear boys' dresses, but boys never do that?'
'Do what?'
'They never wear skirts and tops, sleeveless, backless etc.'
'You can do that. Girls do make up, use lipstick, face cream, that you can also use.' She made fun of Joy, teased him.
She knew these are very common and genuine curiosities for him. It was very interesting to read his mind. She offered him the other day while walking on the beach, while sun was setting.
'You can ask whatever you want to . . . anything, absolutely anything . . . personal also.'
Joy smiled,'Anything . . .?'
'Ya, go ahead?'
'Ok, guys get excited sexually when they see girl's cleavage, legs, lips etc . . . what excites girls when they see guys?'
'Sexuality, cuteness, style!' Jyotika replied.
'Ya! Hmm!' Joy sighed.
'Each girl has different a likings, I can speak for myself, the personality as a whole, the smile, cuteness, a soothing good look. I am

a very emotional person, so I appreciate respect in a boy's eyes, care and love. I tell you one thing, this physical attraction is momentary.'

'Hmm.' Joy tried to show that, he agreed with Jyotika.

'Talent plays a big role in impressing someone, it remains for a longer time. If you ask me, more than anything else, I was impressed by Ray because he was an amazing person; his talent for music and writing poems was amazing'.

'And person's behavior? Doesn't that matter?'

'Everything matters, it depends who is looking for what, may be some other girl looks for 'looks' in a person'.

'What's your story? What would you like to see in your girl?'

'Simplicity, honesty may be . . .'

'Liar.' Jyotika said bluntly.

'She shouldn't be beautiful, sexy?' Jyotika instigated him knowingly—unknowingly, where she is heading to.

'That's secondary for me. Primarily, honesty and simplicity, that can impress me, a beautiful girl like you would be my choice. I wish . . .?' Joy stopped and looked at her.

'You can wish, you can dream to have . . . Go ahead make a wish!' Jyotika incited him.

'I wish to have a girl like you as my girl.' Joy said.

There was silence.

Joy broke the silence.

'I was blind, who was excited to see the world. I came to know that vision has limitations. I am the one who is left with less choices.'

'You have a right to wish like everyone else on this earth.' Jyotika was precise, she didn't want to indulge in further discussion on this topic. The conversation was heading to a direction she was not prepared for. She liked him because of Ray. She had made that clear to everyone. She was not ready for this. She wanted to come out from the constant thought of Ray. Joy's company was helping her in that process.

Bosky was unhappy. She wanted to concentrate on music and be with Rainbow band friends. She let Jyotika and Joy be together, mingle and do whatever they wanted to.

She knew Joy was after a rich beautiful bitch, selfish and opportunist. She was sad to see them together all the time. She wished if Joy could pay attention to music and not on Jyotika, they could create magic together.

She was hot, good looking. She touched her body, when she was undressed in bathroom, she saw it completely. If Joy wanted to choose someone, why that person couldn't be her? She had one person in life, that is Joy; they had grown together, dreamt together, sung together, danced together in each others' arms. She recalled that. Yes . . . always whenever the music started, they used to sing . . .

Feeling high . . .

Me flying in the sky
Let me realize
who am I . . .

She sang the first line 'Me . . . feeling high' and Joy followed second, 'Let me realize who am I . . .'. They created pin-drop silence in music room when they sang.

The other day, when they were without vision, the sky was cloudy. She could feel the air was wet with moisture, breeze forecasting it would rain, the thunder motivated them to sing . . . Joy began that song, full of excitement . . . the rain drops hit the soil, she could feel the cold shooting wind entering the wide open, huge entrance at them, where they used to practice. The smell of dust mixed water hit her nose with pleasant romance. She felt the vibration inside the entire body. She was thrilled, nature was engrossing her into something. She heard Joy was singing 'Lost again . . .'

'Come on,

Show me the way
I am lost again.
Come on Show me the way,
I am lost again . . .
Dust in my eyes
Blind sight
Dark night
And I am looking for you . . .
Hoo woo you . . .
Come on' . . .

The song finished with Shubh's drumbeats. Joy sang the song with immense pain and with true emotion. Bosky felt the silence after the song finished.

'You made us cry.' Ray said in appreciation, his voice became husky as if he was about to cry. He became emotional. He hugged Joy.

Ray had composed this song with saxophone, drum and guitar with mild beats of slow rhythm.

Bosky moved and hugged him too, a tight hug in front of everyone present in the music room. She heard the sound of everyone's claps.

Those were the days when she could do everything with passion and everyone appreciated that.

Those moments had vanished because of Ray's death or because she had got eyes, she had to figure it out. She lost the sympathy, those helping hands, those helping touches of her friends who were always around her, ready to show and hold her hand to step up. She was missing all that. Shubh was the one who was attracted to her and many a times she could feel an extra touch. She responded him with a smile, that's what she did with everyone.

Why couldn't she go with Shubh? She had second thought for a while. He was a good guy too. She pursued, but it didn't work out. Shubh was ready to come closer. He knew that Joy is interested in Jyotika and not Bosky.

It didn't work out. The strong grip of emotions stopped Bosky. Joy might justify himself thinking that, she had chosen Shubh, so what, he did the same by choosing Jyotika. She wouldn't let him do that. In this life, Joy had to come back to her one day.

Menka noticed both of them. She compromised with life and wanted to live a life with this team and music. She couldn't afford to lose Joy and Bosky. For her, they were like two eyes. Yes. Ray's eyes had been donated to them. For that, Dr. R. K. Anand had faced many problems like donating eyes to a known donor, disclosing the identity of both, the donor and the donee. Dr. Anand was questioned by authorities, why did he break the rule of medical ethics.

"Why did you donate eyes to someone who is relative or friend?"
"Eye should be donated to the needy who is already listed in the waiting list, why then you didn't follow the rule?"

Dr. Anand replied and satisfied the committee.

"I have treated the case as exception, we can't beat the drum every time in the name of rules, ethics. I did it for a mother whose young son has lost life; and there is no one else in her family except these 'two' whom the eyes have been donated. By breaking the rule, I have honored the last wish of a person, who did not live even half of his life. As doctor, I have been serving the society since last fifty eight years. I knew Ray who was working for blinds and brought Joy and Bosky from an orphanage. Having helped them, the mother will have a family of three; and she would feel that her son is with her. And I am ready to face any consequences, but if you ask me I am proud of what I did."

The members from the committee knew Dr. Anand is a fighter for the right cause. He should be admired for what he did. Many felt that way. One of the member from the committee had tears, when she came to know the truth of Musical band and mother Menka.

But everyone from the committee was not satisfied with Dr. Anand's reply. "Ok, what would you say for those two visually challenged who missed the chance, despite being in waiting list for years".
"Two visually challenged, needy persons have got vision. Please look everything from that perspective. The glass is half full. I request all of you to be positive in our approach. We are doctors and we see what is the best for people whom we serve." They had no option but to shut the case without any conclusion, for the time being.

Menka thanked Dr. Anand having tears in her eyes.

She knew that Bosky's feelings for Joy were the root cause of the problem between them. She tried to make her understand that, "In life, who makes compromises lives happily." She told Bosky that, she could change herself, but couldn't change the other person. Bosky many times pretended that she understood everything. But she remained adamant.

14

Sunny went to Panchgani alone as he needed time for introspection. He was slightly disturbed by the whole thing and was looking for peace of mind. He also consulted one Guruji who suggested him to wear some stones on his fingers. After four days he was fed up of being alone.

He came back home and called Jyotika.

Jyotika as usual was busy with her musical group and Menka. That day it was raining outside, Bosky found Joy sitting alone. Bosky made coffee for him. Joy smiled, had a sip of coffee looking constantly outside at the rain.

'How is coffee?' Bosky initiated the conversation.

'It's fine, thanks.' Bosky looked at him with love.

'I wanted to say something . . .'

'What are you waiting for? Go ahead and why are you behaving so strange these days? Do you need any permission to say something? What's wrong with you?' Joy said with irritation.

He had noticed that she had become very dictating after they got vision and had started doubting about his whereabouts. Joy did not like this. She never understood that individual space is very important.

'Joy, remember, we have always been together, but now I feel that, we are not that close, you do not have time for me now.'

'Our life has changed, it is not the same, Bosky! Rays eyes have changed our lives! Now we not only can make music, but also can see and feel the rainbow.'

He moved ahead, went to the window and showed her the rainbow which was then in the sky. Bosky followed him; both were standing at the window seeing rainbow.

'Whether you see rainbow or not, the colors of rainbow will remain unchanged, you have to understand that.'

Bosky was angry, irritated, she went inside the room, she had tears in her eyes, she knew that she had lost him. Rains had taken over Mumbai, business had become dull and the entire city was wet. Raincoats, umbrellas were hanging out right from the tea stall to liquor shop, People were busy doing rainy season shopping from these shops, the music room was on the hills of Bandra, a place wherefrom one side sea link was visible and on the otherside, one could see greenery. Jyotika was standing alone, remembering the first time Ray took her there on her birthday.

'I will give you a surprise on your birthday.' Ray had said.

'I know you are not that kind of a person who is going to give a gift.' Jyotika doubted.

'I will show you something, this is more than a gift . . .'

'Show me what?'

'Have patience.' On Jyotika's birthday, Ray took her at the top of the hill with eyes closed, he pulled off the black ribbon and showed the place where she was standing today, the same place . . .She still remembered the conversation she had at that time with Ray, the only difference was, today it looked even more beautiful because of raindrops, the birds were full of energy and ready to explore, jump and fly.

'So the only surprise you wanted to give me was this high and top place?' Ray held her hand gently and took her inside. That was a cave like place where musical instruments were kept and his friends were practicing music.

'Isn't this place a surprise?' Ray's voice resounded. She was welcomed by everyone.

Manoj insisted her to sing rainbow song, Rehman tried to impress her with his guitar, she felt like a princess, yes that was Ray's palace and kingdom which might have impressed her so much that, everything became insignificant and tasteless after that.

Ray had a great team and the team loved him too.
'Whose place is this? Who owns this place?' Jyotika had asked.
'No one . . .' Ray had replied.
'This BMC land has been encroached by a builder called Khan Bhai. We started practising here without any intimation. At first Khan Bhai was very angry when he heard about it, he came with his men to throw us out.

We were practsing rainbow at that time.

He heard the music and he was happy with it! He not only allowed us to practice music here, but also he is now ready to invest in our Rainbow project'. Manoj explained. Ray was like that, anybody could get impressed except her father. He was a genius. Joy, meanwhile came there, she came back from the trans.
'Why are you standing alone here, let's go inside.' Joy said. Both of them smiled looking at each other, Joy's hand was wrapped around her waist and both went inside to see the practice. Rehman was playing guitar, Vandy was singing and Manoj was playing keyboard. Jyotika suddenly felt that the music was sounding lifeless.
'Stop the music! What are you doing? What's wrong with you Manoj? It's not coming out properly.' Jyotika said in high pitched voice.

Bosky was already irritated; she could not take it when she saw Jyotika talking like that.
'Manoj, why did you stop the music?' Bosky confronted. She was ready for a fight. She didn't care what would happen next.
'You are the music director, not she! She has no idea what music is! I am the singer and I know what music is, she cannot dictate terms like that; and if she thinks she can, I am not going to take it!'

Everybody was shocked.
'What are you saying? Have you lost it?' Rehman tried to set it right, 'You have gone out of your mind, not me!'

Bosky was not ready to listen this time, she wanted to explode all her anger.

'She had been dating Sunny and now she is with Joy! If Sunny comes in her life it's fine or else Joy is there for her! She has snatched Joy from me'.

'What Rubbish! She is showing me things I wanted to see' Joy defended.

'I know what she is doing; and I also know what you are seeing. I know what is she SHOWING TO YOU . . . ! I know the drama! I know what is happening behind my back. She will leave you one day alone Joy; and then don't come to me. I have had enough Joy. I am happy that you have changed, I am happy to know a new Joy, who left me for somebody . . . I do not want a guy who will leave me for someone else, I want somebody who can be with me for lifetime and you are not like that'

She was just burning with anger and wanted to explode. There was pin-drop silence for a second.

Joy saw tears in Jyotika's eyes. But she was calm and firm. 'Rainbow was Ray's dream, he has got you here. This place belongs to Ray, not you; and one more thing, today if both of you can see, it's because of Ray only! He has given vision to your lives. But it's OK, I am wasting my time here, I have no more business to do here, it's time to move ahead . . .'

Jyotika left. Everyone was silent; jealousy had spoiled everything. They knew that sometimes being silent is the best solution.

*N*aina was about to leave the Police Station when Rawat approached her. He had gone somewhere since afternoon.

'What is it?' She smiled looking at Rawat, she knew that Rawat had got some evidence and he had something to say.

'I have got some very important evidence.'

'About Which case you are talking now?'

'You remember the young man, who had been killed at footpath, 'Ray'. That music guy.'

'Oh yes, I do.'

'I have got the evidence; there was a CC-TV camera outside the jewelry shop. I have got the footage of that Camera. The driver was standing there near the truck. It seems he was observing and waiting for Ray. The moment the driver saw Ray stepping on the footpath, he started the truck and drove on the footpath, hit him, which resulted in death of this young man. I think there was some issue between Ray and driver. Ray was hit against the tree.'

'No, there wasn't any issue between them; the driver was hired to kill Ray. But the question is who wanted to kill Ray? Someone had given money to the driver to kill Ray.'

Inspector Naina then decided to meet Sunny who was one of the closest friends of Ray's girlfriend. She knew that this murder had some connection with Jyotika's life and there were big people involved; after all Sunny was a known businessman.

Sunny was cool when he was replying the question.

'Mr. Sunny I thought you can help me in solving this case.' Ray was Jyotika's friend, and I will be very happy to help you. Would you like to have some tea or coffee?'

'Coffee will be fine.' That's Naina Muke; her style would never let anyone know what is in her mind. She became friendly to everyone very fast.

The peon appeared in a minute.
Took note of whatever Sunny said and left gently.

'Jyotika was Ray's girlfriend?'
'That's true she was his girlfriend.'
'Did you know this?'
'Yes, I did.'
'Jyotika is your childhood friend. You wanted to marry her, but she did not; wasn't it a difficult time for you?' Naina had come after a research work.
'Obviously it was not a very pleasant moment for me initially, but I love her and when you love someone you want that person to be happy.'

Sunny's answer was balanced, no excitement, no anger; he was very cool when he was replying. He was scared but he was able to maintain his cool.

The coffee was served in an expensive tray. The tray was very clean. The boy was keeping the cup. Secretary Monica was observing standing there, that everything should fall in place without any mistake. Naina noticed that his office was well organized and it showed whatever Sunny does, does it with proper planning.

'What's your opinion about this case?'
'Which case?' Sunny asked her looking into her mind.
'Ray's case; that he has been murdered.'

'I am no one to speak about this case, since you are asking me, the bigger question is why? Why someone would kill him? He was a simple musician trying to come up with his music.'

Naina listened with patience. She finished the coffee.

'Thank for your time Mr. Sunny.'
'You came here without any warrant and I cooperated. But please remember for the next time, you will see my lawyer before talking to me.' Naina smiled and looked straight in his eyes.

She left without uttering a word.
She knew what she was doing.

She had a definite strategy for a high profile case like that.
The police jeep was running on the road. People used to pay attention to police jeep especially when there is female police officer. She was used to this.

This was a very important case; very important for her career as big people were involved in this case.

Ray, a young guy, devoted all his life for blinds, the killer must be very ruthless or it was a simple case of accident?

But CC tv camera footage hinted a conspiracy.
She had to find it out!

Koyal was upset and angry. It was insulting for her that, the police came in their office and enquired like that. If this news was leaked to media, then it would have affected their business. Koyal called the PR department and instructed them that, there should not be a single news against the company. She could not sleep that night. What was happening in her life?

Why did police inspector knock her office?
What was wrong?
Why did police choose to question Sunny?
Something, somewhere was wrong.

Next day, Jyotika was at home for whole day. She didn't want to go anywhere and she also didn't want to meet anyone. She had food in the afternoon and had siesta around four thirty.

She got up, had tea and still just wanted to be at herself. She didn't come out from her bedroom. She took that diary which she had brought from Ray's house after his demise.
The diary was full of Ray's poetry . . .

Jyotika was inside her bedroom till late night.
Jyotika's parents were worried seeing Jyotika like that.
They called up Sunny and his family for a small get-together. Charu went inside Jyotika's bedroom and told her that, Sunny had come to see her. Jyotika was happy to see Sunny; it was a bit relaxing getting out of all those thoughts of Bosky, Joy and the entire music room event.

Sunny and Jyotika went for a walk in the night. For Sunny that was the greatest moment of his life. He felt that night Jyotika was truly with him, only with him . . .

'How is Rainbow going on?' Sunny asked looking deep inside the dark night at Worli sea face. Normally sea face was crowded in the evening, but late night it looks deserted, calm and a peaceful place where, one can have a peaceful walk. 'Music is fine, but I am not a musician . . . I am just supporting them.' She did not want to discuss this topic again.

There was silence between them for a while.

'Hmm . . . how was your day?' She changed the subject.
'The police inspector came to know more about Ray's accident.'
'How stupid! Ray met with an accident,' she reacted instantly.
Sunny didn't say anything. He knew that nothing can be done about it.
'She was doing her duty.' Sunny said.

Jyotika knew that Sunny was going through a tough phase.
She should support Sunny instead of supporting the stupid musical group. She found herself lost without Ray in this world. She had done her best to come out of it; but at the end of the day she was blamed with maligned intention. And on the other hand, there was somebody who

cared for her so much. It was so stupid of her leaving him all alone, she needed some time to think.

'Aunty was telling that you go nowhere these days, not even for music practice.' Sunny started the topic again.

'I need some change. Honestly speaking Sunny, everything was, and is because of Ray, Ray has gone and things are no longer the same.' She said with little irritation.

Sunny became very happy after hearing that. God had listened to him. May be the stone he was wearing was effective and had started yielding results. Thanks to Guruji! He thought of calling him to convey thanks.

Sunny went home, had bath and had some champagne. He used to have it when he was very happy. He called his Guruji but he was sleeping. One of his disciples told him to call the next day.

Early in the morning next day, there was a call from Guruji. He was very happy and told Sunny that everything will be fine in his life now. Sunny invited Guruji home, early morning on Sunday.

Next morning, Jyotika went to his office to surprise Sunny, but Sunny had not come to the office. He was at home. Koyal invited her in her cabin, they had coffee together.

'How are you Jyotika?'

'Very well, what about you?'

'So what's happening in music, Rainbow . . .if I remember it correctly?'

'Nothing much . . .'

'You know, I loved music throughout my life but, now just office and home'.

'I know things change what to do?' She gave her cold and standard answer.

There was silence for a moment.

Jyotika did not want to discuss music.

Koyal and Jyotika were discussing men then. Jyotika came to know that Koyal was a fantastic person. She was very cheerful. She shared lots of jokes. She actually had very good time with her. Jyotika saw Sunny's pictures on Koyal's mobile screen, both of them were together and laughing, but Jyotika was shocked to see that,

'Shall I ask you a personal question? What do you think about Sunny?' Jyotika asked.

'What do you mean? I didn't get your question?'

'Generally, I am asking generally, in case if you were at my place and if you had to take decision about Sunny, as life partner, what decision would you have taken?' Jyotika threw a bomb.

Koyal was shocked hearing that question. She never thought this will come from Jyotika. She didn't know what to say. Very Next moment Koyal thought this is the chance, she could make Jyotika realize that she is not the only girl in Sunny's life.

'I wish I could be at your place sweetheart, life would have been much easier with Sunny. Sunny is a fantastic man,' Koyal said winking at Jyotika naughtily. 'It's a hypothetical question, difficult for me to answer, who would have been my choice?'

'Just think casually and tell me.' Jyotika again asked.

'If you insist, I wouldn't have delayed a second to choose him.' Koyal replied.

Jyotika smiled, did not say anything and went back home. Jyotika was thinking about Sunny's relationship with Koyal. Koyal is tall, pretty, sexy and successful. She has no boyfriend, she spends all the time with Sunny. Is she dating Sunny?

Has Sunny been attracted to Koyal? Are they in a relationship? Has she actually lost Sunny? Or Sunny is double dating?

Is it too late for her to go to Sunny? Why is she thinking about Sunny? She has no clear direction, which way to go?' She first had to decide whom to choose and then . . . she stopped thinking as she was confused.

16

*J*yotika found herself all alone.

She didn't know where to lead. She didn't even know whom she loved, with whom she wanted to be . . . It was a bizarre situation, Ray had gone and she was left with a dilemma. She reached home, had lunch and went to sleep again.

In the evening, when she got up, she overheard Sunny's voice; he was talking to her mom. Jyotika was wearing shorts. She came out of her room.

Sunny had gone to meet his Guruji, and then his office guys told him that Jyotika had come there to meet him, so he came home to meet Jyotika. Charu left both of them in the living room and went inside. Sunny smiled.

'So, you were sleeping.'
'You have developed a habit of saying 'so' frequently. Jyotika said little lightly. Their relationship was formal. They never behaved like close friends.
'No . . . I mean, I don't know . . . May be, what can I say?'

Jyotika was looking so very beautiful in shorts. The light coming from window was falling straight on her legs and waist; her fair beautiful hands were fascinating him. Her face was very graceful. Sunny wished if he could kiss her now, could he? Or, was it the right time? How would she react? Would she respond? He was not sure.

He had kissed Koyal. She was amazing. A kiss is always amazing . . . Koyal was fine, but Jyotika . . . she was a stunning beauty!

'I went to your office to meet you; you were not there, so I came back, had lunch and hit the bed.'

'Hmm . . . I know, I am coming from office only.' Sunny always had cold answers like that, very formal.

Sunny was a different kind of a person from Ray, very different.

Ray was cozy, very naughty, he used to kiss her, hold her, hug her tight. Sometimes she felt suffocated, unable to breathe.

'What's wrong with you, is this a way hold a girl' she became angry that day, at Ray's home.

'Tell me how to hold a girl?' He said and hold her again tight.

'Like This?' He tightened his clutch 'like this?, Is this fine.' She was unable to move. Her body was so tightly held by him that, she thought she would die in a second or few moments. Ray freed her from his clutch after a few moments when he found that she had problem breathing.

The moment she was free she took a long breathe, Ray was laughing like an idiot. She was irritated.

She slapped him tight.

It was hard, very hard. He was shocked. His laughter vanished immediately.

'I could've died you beast.' She shouted at him.

'Will you ever learn how to touch a girl.' Ray was silent his cheek was red.

He was silent and blank, perhaps he never thought she could slap him like this.

'I would never touch you again.' He was angry.

'Oh, look who is talking as if you do a faver by touching me.' She reacted sharply.

'Yes I do.'

'Great, good for me, good for you.'

After half an hour he prepared tea for himself, and didn't even ask whether she would like to have or not, he was ready for the fight. He took his guitar to play.

'Ok, I am leaving.' Jyotika was in no mood to continue.

'I didn't invite you, you came on your own, you are a free bird, whom no one can touch, I will not touch even after marrying you.'

'Who is getting married with you? Me? Never, never to an idiot like you. You would kill me on my first night. And I do not want to be killed on my first night'.

He laughed on my sense of humor. He jumped and hugged me softly.

'Is this hug ok?'

'You can hug me slightly tight that's also fine.'

'He put his lips on her lips and pressed that.'

'I asked you to hug not to kiss boy.'

Both sipped tea from the same cup, one by one with love and romance flavoured in it.

Smile appeared on her lips, thinking of those precious moments, she really missed Ray and his love.

Ray was wild, vibrant and energetic.

He was one in a million.

'Where are you lost?'

She heard Sunny's voice.

'Nowhere . . .' she replied flatly.

'Did you meet Koyal today?' Sunny asked.

'I met Koyal, had a chat with her. Nice girl! I have met her before, but never got a chance to know her. She has become my friend now. She also has a habit of saying 'So', have you noticed that?'

'Ohh! Really? I never noticed that,' Sunny lied.

You never noticed? You lair! That's your problem, you do not notice anything in life. Just lie. Double dater. She knew the secret of his life now. Boys will be boys, cheating innocent girls like her.

She was pissed off! She felt like slapping Sunny. She thought she had snatched the mask from his face!
Sunny was double faced, she knew.
'We are partners in the business. She left modeling and joined me, loaded with investment, in my early days, you must be aware of that.' Sunny clarified.

You both are partners in crime. The crime you both have committed is to cheat me. She thought. What an idiot I am, who doesn't know this elderly looking person, having innocence on his face can cheat people.

She found Joy was more like Ray, the same cute smile, fair color . . . She really had a very good time with Joy telling him about this world. She remembered, one day when she was with Joy on the beach, he was asking the difference between sand and soil. Even she was not knowing the basic difference between them, she tried to explain that,

'Sand is like sand, it shines. Sand has less density than soil. You can grow something on soil but not on sand. You can find sand besides sea, where there is lot of water. But the most interesting thing is when you dig the sand deep beneath you will find different kind of soil.'

'I am not understanding this, but it's fine. What I can touch and feel that, sand is hard and soil is soft.' Joy was so precise!

And what a fantastic singer he is!
When he sings Rainbow, he dissolves himself in it . . .,

Me feeling high,
Flying in the sky,
Let me realize who am I,
Who I am . . .

This song is so very connected to her heart. It was one of the best songs in her memory and she simply loved the music.

'What are you thinking?' Sunny was asking something.

She was always in thoughts of someone else whenever she was with Sunny, always! Yes, she realized it again. Sunny was an introvert person having a mask on his face.

He never showed his reality to anyone.

Sunny's voice broke her thought cycle. Sunny was looking at her and talking something about business and she was actually not listening to him, lost in her own thoughts.

'I am sorry, I was thinking something, did you say something?' She wanted to ask him to get lost! Get out from her house immediately.

She was really engaged in her thoughts, that she could only see Sunny's lip movements.

Sunny was slightly nervous when he felt that she was with him but her mind was somewhere else, he felt ignored! But he could understand her state of mind and the reason, why she is occupied with so many thoughts, Sunny revived again,

'I was saying that, we will go somewhere for a long drive if you wish.'
'Where?'
'Anywhere!' Sunny replied.
'I am not a gypsy Sunny.' Jyotika was straight.

She was pissed off. Anywhere? Goa, Kashmir, forest, valley, lake . . . She would commit suicide, rather than traveling with him. She didn't want that. They were two different people. And now when she knew that, he had a secret, he had a girlfriend, she was never going to go with Sunny anywhere. She noticed he had stone rings in three of his fingers.

Pratap Sanyal entered and became very happy to see Sunny with his daughter.
'Oh! Oh! What a pleasant surprise! I am very happy to see you both together. Are you going somewhere?'

'We are making plans. Ok, let's go for a movie.' Sunny was quick in his answer. He didn't miss the chance; he knew in front of Uncle, she couldn't have refused.

'We can watch a play if you want.' Jyotika never watched a film.

'Yes, we can. Which play?'

'We will decide when we reach there in the theatre.'

'Sure.' Sunny didn't want 'Prithvi' but it was ok.

Jyotika wanted to give some time to herself.

She wanted to think and introspect. She went inside to get ready, she saw herself in mirror, her face was glowing. She looked at the portrait given by Menka. Ray was singing in front of her, she posed the same looking at him.

She wore pink top and black skirt, one of her very favorite dresses.

'How do I look?' She asked looking at Ray's painting.

'You look beautiful . . . Very beautiful, sexy!' She said to herself, pretending that Ray is saying.

She smiled.

'Why are you going with this doubled faced, idiot?' She says again changing her voice.

'Because you have gone long, leaving me alone, and Bosky is fighting with me, what should I do?' She changed the voice again. She said and left the room.

Sunny was blank when he saw her talking to a poster. A dead portrait! She suddenly felt embarrassed to see him at the door.

'I was getting bored, uncle insisted me to go inside your room, sorry!' He was little nervous. 'Good poster, Oh! It's Ray,' Sunny saw it closely.

'Ray's mom had gifted it to me. I see him every morning when I get up.'

Both of them went to see the play. Jyotika was talking all her way about music, power of music, theatre, play, cinema and her interest in doing creative things. The play started in time. Both of them enjoyed the play till late night, had dinner outside and reached home around 12

O'clock at night. Worli sea face was as calm as it happened to be in the midnight, both of them started walking.

'You know what pure creativity is? When soil melts down with water and produces greenery everywhere; green trees, leaves, flying birds, running animals, flowing waters, endless sea, rains, this is pure creativity! When I see nature I go mad, I listen to the rhythm of nature, it has some meaning.'

Jyotika kept on talking; but Sunny was not amazed to listen to all that boring and old stuff.

'She always tries to be different with nature. A changed definition of creativity, bullshit! She is good for nothing. Jyotika will never change.' Sunny was irritated. She was always in some other thoughts, whenever she was with him. She talked of Ray who was dead.

'See, the sea surface and the moonlight on water; when I see it I actually feel it, I like merging myself with this part of nature . . .'

She kept on talking She was lost in nature, Sunny was listening to her without saying a word. He thought, 'she has gone really mad and there is no point in wasting time behind her.' But he wanted to ask Guruji first, what he was supposed to do in such a situation.

'Jyotika, will you come to my house on Sunday, this Sunday?'
'Look at this idiot, she is talking about such an important thing, he didn't utter a word and now he is asking me to come to his house! What rubbish!'
'Is there anything special?' She asked.
'I know one Swami Guruji. He has given me these stones. He always helped me growing my business. And now I want you to meet him.'
'I will see if I can make it? When is Sunday?'
'Day after tomorrow.' Sunny was hopeful.

Next morning Jyotika got up late, at around 10:45 O'clock. She saw many missed calls from Joy and messages requesting her to call back. She felt like calling him back. She looked at Ray's portrait.

'Should I call him or not?' She asked looking at the portrait. 'Ok, fine I should go.' She decided as if Ray had consented.

Bosky might be against her, but that was not her fault. She was jealous and that was her problem. But if Jyotika didn't go to the team, they would have felt devastated; everyone would have suffered because of Bosky and it was not at all a good idea! She convinced herself.

Joy sent another message,

'Hw r u? Plz cm.'

'We all miss you, please come.' Menka's sms was relieving, she became tension-free.

She was also missing the entire group.

17

*S*he got a call from Sunny, but did not attend that. Why she didn't want to talk to Sunny? Answer may be anything, but she was not ready to ponder upon it then. She knew that her relationship with Sunny would never work. It might make everyone happy; except her!

Sunny was not her type of guy; Stones, Guruji . . . According to her, he was living in an artificial world, where things were controlled by astrologers. There was no doubt about it that she didn't want him in her life.

She decided to get fresh.

She had a glass of water, entered the bathroom and started thinking again, if Ray would have been alive, there would have been no second thought. But choosing between Sunny and this group is really not so difficult; she had to choose Joy because Joy was Ray for her!

Jyotika wanted to stop thinking, but she couldn't. She started brushing her teeth.

She actually wanted to help Rainbow, so that Ray's dream could be fulfilled, she justified herself having shower, while cooling herself down. The decision was made, there was nothing like love, she was supporting the mission, she had a purpose in life, working for the noble cause; and through this noble cause, she wanted to achieve Ray's unfulfilled dream too.

Jyotika came out in white soft bathrobe to select the dress. What was to be worn? It was a big question, she struggled to make this decision every morning! Blue jeans and white T-shirt, final!

Now what? To whom should she call? Joy?

Jyotika was tired of taking such decisions. Moreover she had to face another problem, her mom was waiting for her for breakfast. She would barge in anytime asking to eat something. She was not feeling hungry, but she had to eat. It was different situation altogether. When she was in the musical group, everyone listened to her. She used to place orders for whenever she wanted to eat, no one used to force her to eat. Not like her mother who was after her life; she felt free when she was with the group. She got another sms from Joy,

'Bosky is regretting, feeling sorry. Please come, everyone is waiting for you, me too.' "Me too" she reads the message again. Great! So, should she call Joy first. She would call Sunny too, but later, not now.

The decision was taken.

She took the car key and left home. Everyone welcomed her, Bosky also regretted for her behavior. She was accepted as a leader as Ray was. She felt proud of herself that, she had done at least something meaningful in life. The day went on just like that, evening took over with darkness. She forgot to call Sunny. Sunny called up many times, but she was busy and couldn't take his call.

At Night, when Jyotika came back, Sunny was waiting for her in her own house, with her parents on the dinner table.

'I am so sorry Sunny; I couldn't take your call as I was in a music session.'
Sunny didn't say a word. He was hurt. Jyotika was his lifeline and she even didn't have time to call him back! What was he doing? Just wasting his time! Jyotika didn't love him. She would never change; her love was music team-Rainbow.

'Let's go for a walk' Sunny asked her casually after dinner. Jyotika had hardly eaten anything.

She was scared if she didn't eat at all, her mom would have ask millions of questions. She didn't have energy to walk, but she had to. Sometimes we have to do such things to make others happy!

Sky was dark that night.
Silence had gripped both of them. Nothing was there to talk. Sunny breathed and smiled looking at her.
'What about tomorrow? Are you free?'
'We will discuss it tomorrow Sunny, I do not know if anything crops up, and I do not want you to wait, honestly speaking.' The reply was crystal clear. She said right on his face not to wait, to leave her alone.

Sunny knew, he had lost her, but whenever he was alone, he used to think about it over and over again. He believed that, no matter what she is up to but the power of Guruji would set everything right. So it was no waste of time, but an investment.

Power of positive thinking says, "No matter what, but you have to believe in yourself and keep trying hard, hard on everything; one day success will fall at your feet".

Sunny had followed this principle till date. He knew he had to had patience. He still believed in his principles and the stones were also of help. Plus, he knew Guruji would never fail.

'As you say, see your music session shouldn't be disturbed,' Sunny said and left soon after that.

Jyotika entered home, and found that her dad was waiting for her. She had really no energy to talk to them. He looked at her having lots of question marks on forehead.

She moved fast in her room and straight under the shower wearing clothes.

This was her way to release stress.

The next day Sunny didn't go anywhere, it was anyways holiday. He slept for whole day. He knew that Jyotika would not call him. She might be busy with music.

Koyal called him in the evening; he said he wanted to be at home. Koyal came home. Sunny's face was pale, sad, he looked disappointed. He was lying in the bedroom when Koyal entered. He got up and hugged her. It wasn't as normal as it used to be, for some time both of them kept on hugging each other. He felt good. A hug, has a power. It makes one comfortable. After a moment Sunny left her body and breathed. She didn't leave fully, she looked into Sunny's eyes and moved her face close to him, Sunny moved his face too. He knew some moments are special; he responded to Koyal's kiss, both of them kept on kissing for some time. Koyal closed the door and they were ready to begin a new journey!

He lost himself in Koyal's love making. She removed her clothes. His hands went behind Koyal's back, he saw Jyotika smiling . . . Yes! He saw Jyotika's photograph.

Sunny saw Koyal without cloths; she had such an amazing body! A model, who left career for him. Both of them saw Jyotika's photograph. Love happens sooner or later! And there is no harm in getting involved physically; they knew it. If two people want to get involved, they will, sooner or later!

Sunny's car was talking to darkness. Koyal was happy; satisfied, composed and calm. She felt complete! She couldn't see Sunny in sad mood. He was the best! She knew it, but stupid enough to follow a girl who doesn't love him.

They drank till late night at Koyal's flat. Sunny couldn't get back home in time next day, when Swami Guruji was waiting for him since early morning, talking to his Dad. Sunny went home with Koyal.

'She is the right girl whom you love from childhood.' Swami Guruji made an announcement seeing Koyal with Sunny.

Later, when he was informed that she was another girl named Koyal, his business partner, Guruji became nervous and the situation was very embarrassing. Sunny was confused, how Guruji could make this kind of mistake, he claimed himself at par with God and that, he knew everything.

His father Mohan, then, made him understand that even God can make mistakes.

'What is the possibility of Jyotika and Sunny's marriage?' Mohan Kumar asked Guruji.

'Hundred percent!' Guruji said.

They knew that once Guruji said it, means it would definitely happen. On Monday, Sunny attended the office with fresh and happy mood. He never wanted to be physical with Koyal, but she did it knowingly, so it was not his fault then! Late at night when everyone had left, the security was waiting to shut the office, Koyal came in his cabin and said with a smile, 'Let's go for dinner.'

'Ok, let's go.' Both of them went for dinner.

18

That entire week was hectic, very hectic.

Jyotika was busy with the entire group having fun, making new tunes. Most of the times she was with Joy. He was sweet, unaware of other side of the life . . . Jyotika came very close to Joy these days.

The entire group had accepted their intimacy without a question. Bosky had accepted the fact that, she would lose even Joy's friendship if she would try to get him by force. Bosky was quiet.

She had decided to keep herself busy with music. She either always practiced to enhance her voice quality or played guitar. Menka helped her to join the musical Gharana of Pandit Yashpal Sharma, she began to learn classical music and started practicing day and night.

Joy was occupied with Jyotika, in knowing and understanding life.

He sometimes felt insecure as he knew that, Jyotika was rich and moody and one day she might go away from him.

'Do not leave me ever Jyotika, never ever leave me, promise me!'
'Why do you think I will leave you Joy?' Joy had no answer. He looked at her; Jyotika moved ahead and hugged him.

'You sing really well, I love your singing. I am your fan, a huge fan Joy! Why would I leave you? I can't leave my cute singing friend ever.'

Joy blushed listening so much of praises. Joy's eyes reminded her of Ray. Simple guy, always wearing T-shirt and jeans, no money, no home, just a singer! He didn't even know where he belonged to . . . An orphanage!

Jyotika felt good when joy was singing. She loved his innocence; she loved Joy! She had feelings for him. She had fallen in love with Joy.

She forgot everything when she was with Joy. Day, night, morning, evening, all the time! He was like Ray only. The other day, Jyotika drove down to a mall with joy, to buy stuff for music room. Joy was looking at the light all the time. 7-8 hours vanished with him, explaining things and buying T-shirts for him. Menka and everyone began calling them. When they came back Jyotika brought a bundle of clothes and an expensive cellphone for Joy, everyone was speechless including Joy. They knew Ray's girlfriend is now Joy's girl.

'I feel jealous!' Manoj commented with a smile.

'Don't be jealous. I have brought T-shirts for everyone.' Jyotika said with a smile, she was blushing too. The love was obvious and overt.

'Let's party now!' Vandy opened a bottle of wine and snacks packet. The party began. Music was playing.

Everyone was in a good mood. Joy was little high after drinking liquor. He was like that! Joy tossed the coin and said 'Heads she loves me, tails I love her,' everyone laughed at him. Shubh whistled.

They enjoyed party till late night, late till two am. Joy took her in his arms, danced and kissed finally when they were alone in balcony.

Pratap and Charu waited till late night for Jyotika. She entered home at around 2:50 am. She was drunk.

'I was partying papa with the Rainbow team; will talk tomorrow; will discuss everything you want.' Jyotika hugged her dad and said. She went to bed.

Next morning before they could say anything Jyotika announced, 'I love Joy.' They were shocked.

'Who is Joy? I thought she is in love with Sunny; she was going out with him, meeting him these days.' Pratap was shocked!

'Joy is in the same musical group. He was blind, fortunately Ray donated his one eye to him and another to Bosky; and so he has a vision now! He can see with one eye.' Jyotika explained.

'Sorry? How one person can donate eyes to two different individuals?' He couldn't understand anything.

'One person's eyes donated to two people.' Jyotika explained this time.

This girl is stupid! She doesn't understand anything. This happens when someone gets everything at home without having earned a penny. Daughter of a rich person spoiling reputation and business of the family for music. Stupid girl! Has no respect for her parents, especially for her dad. This generation is selfish anyways; ruthless, emotionless! She has got everything she wanted, everything! Whatever she wanted to study, whatever brand of car she wanted, she has it; even the kind of freedom he has given her no parents give nowadays. Pratap couldn't stop regretting.

This marriage will be a great association! Sunny has a secure future; he is handsome, tall, good looking boy, whom she knows since childhood. Leaving this kind of diamond, she loves a boy who has no background, no one knows him; where he is from? An orphan who can see with only one eye!

He knew Jyotika was blind, but others could see and foresee the consequences! He was fed up of her stupid decisions; and that day had lost faith in his wife Charu also! After these incidences, he felt that his wife was good for nothing. He thought she had failed in educating her own kid; she had raised a spoilt kid, making all idiotic decisions.

But, it was entirely his fault also. He had given freedom to his wife and daughter and now everything had been destroyed by his own negligence, he had no hopes for future.

This decision was conveyed to Sunny. He knew it. Sunny's dad Mohan, was completely shaken hearing this decision, he immediately rushed to Pratap Sanyal.

'How can she do that?' Mohan was shocked.

He knew his son was one in a million and girls were standing in que to marry him. Mohan thought the Sanyal family was not a family but a circus wherein Jyotika was playing a joker, spoilt kid! But he was worried about his son, who had loved Jyotika and was ready to leave everything for her . . . Mohan was worried about Sunny; Sunny could do anything as he was madly in love with Jyotika. He was a very emotional guy, a motherless boy, who loved this girl like anything, but she ruined his life. Then Mohan called Guruji and expressed his worry.

Guruji suggested him some rituals, which he performed. He was worried about his only son! Sunny! The only asset he had. If something would happen to him, he would never forgive this circus family . . .full of jokers!

'What should we do now? I have met Guruji, performed whatever he said. Guruji said they should get married soon or else . . .' Mohan said without waiting for a single second.
'Or else?' Pratap asked.
'He predicted that this marriage would bring happiness.' Mohan hid the negative apprehensions of the prediction.
'You don't worry, everything will be alright. Jyotika needs some time to think. She is influenced by the musical team. She is young, enjoying the parties and all that stuff, but this gang of musicians will never be successful in dragging Jyotika in their side, trust me!' Pratap cooled him down.
Charu was sitting besides them and listening to their talk. Charu knew she would never agree to marry Sunny. Jyotika was her daughter. She failed but Jyotika wouldn't.

Mohan Kumar was sure, Guruji would never fail.

Jyotika, on the other hand, had made a statement and now she was not ready to listen to anyone. It was her life and only she could make all the decisions and no one else! Her mother tried to read her mind next morning, 'Are you sure you want to be with Joy and not with Sunny?' Charu asked her making very comfortable in her lap.

'Joy is love of my life and that is final.'

'Do you know this will make many people unhappy?'

'Momma, the question is, why? Why, this will make everyone unhappy? If I will marry somebody else, I will be unhappy; do you want to see me unhappy?' Jyotika questioned back her mom. 'I tried hard to be with Sunny, but he is double faced. He does what his Guruji says. He has no guts. For everything he goes to that Guruji to sort out his problems'. Jyotika exploded.

Charu knew that Jyotika was right. Sunny had developed his business and earned money. He was known as a successful businessman in society; but that didn't mean that Jyotika should marry him. He was unexpressive; she would be suffocated in his company. He couldn't even make his decisions.

'All of you are forcing me just because dad wants to crack a deal! Sunny's dad is looking for a bigger business association, do you think I don't know that? I am old enough to understand these money matters. Do not turn my life into business deals, I am human, do not treat our humane relationship like business tie ups!' She got up and sat right in front of her mom, face to face.

'And please mom, I am seeing enough of assets in my life; cars, bungalows, properties, but now what I am looking in life is happiness. I do not want to hurt you saying this, but since you have started this topic, I have to show you the real picture. I can't be happy with money, I know that, and now you also should know. I have to fulfill Ray's dream. I know dad isn't happy. He is a big businessman and his reputation is on stake. When a half blind person becomes his son-in-law, he will be defeated in his business circle, but I cannot change his thinking!' She stopped for a while.

Ok momma if you were at my place, and you were to take decision, what would you have done? Hadn't you chosen Joy?'

'Our times were more stringent, I wish, I had an opportunity to take such decision.' Charu said with pain. Charu had tears in her eyes.

Jyotika couldn't understand why her mom was in tears.

Next morning . . .

'Nonsense! What is she up to?' Pratap was not only disturbed but divested completely. Jyotika left the breakfast table and went inside the room.

19

*K*oyal was the coolest, she was happy. Is Sunny going to come to her at the end of the day? She was a bit worried knowing that Sunny wants to get married to Jyotika, in spite of whatever happened between them.

Strange man! She was little disturbed with Sunny's behavior. Love sucks! Can't help him anymore. She was left with no choice. She decided to wait and watch.

Koyal was trying to take care of business seriously. The office staff knew something was wrong, fishy! They hardly saw Sunny those days. The company had been nurtured very well with good people. They never questioned integrity of their bosses. They knew that the company had future, so they did not need to worry, as long as they are associated with the company. Jyotika was involved in fulfilling Ray's dream, keeping the marriage aside.

The songs were ready with final dubbing. Seven songs had been shot with well renowned film director and the celebration began. Jyotika threw a huge party in Worli Box, the most happening place, close to Worli sea face. The announcement was made to hype the music album which had seven songs, media was invited for cocktail and dinner. Everyone spoke about Ray and the music and the album was dedicated to Ray. Jyotika made a statement that the profit of the album will benefit the blind schools and eye banks.

Next morning, Jyotika was sleeping till late. All the newspapers covered the news including electronic media, entertainment channels as well as news channels. Early in the morning while having tea, Charu was watching these news alone, Pratap had gone to the office as usual very early. Charu knew that Jyotika would get up at around 11O'clock, she would be very happy seeing all these promotions, she opened the music channels, songs were running almost on all the music channels. Bosky got up in the morning. She found that everyone was sleeping, she was having a headache. She went inside the kitchen to make tea, a strong black tea was a stress-buster for her always.

Last night, she felt like a dream had come true! She had drinks like everyone else, she had no idea how many pegs. There was no tea in the kitchen, Plastic jar which used to have tea was empty. She wokes up Joy for that.

'Will you bring some tea? The tea jar is empty.' Joy wasn't in mood to bring anything but Bosky insisted.

'Please Joy.' Bosky insisted . . .

Joy went outside and started walking on the footpath, he didn't know what happened, but he moved few steps and he was bounced against a lamp-post. Joy started bleeding, fell on the footpath. It was morning time, 07:50 am. Hardly a few people were around there, but some of them took him to the hospital.

20

*J*yotika got the news sharp around 12 O'clock. When she woke up and switched her phone on, there were many missed calls and messages about Joy's accident. She rushed to the hospital, he had head injury, he was resting in the hospital, but fortunately he was fine.

Inspector Naina visited the location of that accident. The truck hit Joy in the same way as it hit Ray before. Rawat and Naina noted all the details of the crime scene. This time the driver had died on the spot. It seemed that he couldn't control the truck. The front tires of the truck missed the point, the driver wanted to touch, it went on the other side of the footpath which was too high and it tumbled losing its balance. Joy was hit for sure, but not from the front. The driver fell down from the driver's seat and crashed beneath the truck's body. One dead, one injured! The crane pulled the truck; and the dead body of the driver was taken for postmortem.

Later, she came to know that this driver was the same, who killed Ray. The dash board of the truck had similar envelope, this time having Rs.50,000 cash inside it. Case was clear! Someone had paid to kill Joy. But who?

21

*I*nspector Naina started a fresh investigation, she revised the entire case papers and decided to meet each and every person, who was associated with this case. She knew that there was some conspiracy involved! A young chap was killed, after that another attempt of murder; and the suspect is dead. But the case was not closed. Someone had conspired the entire plot and he was doing it very smartly. She wanted to reach at the core of the case.

Inspector Naina met Joy and recorded his statement. Joy was in the hospital and survived with minor injuries. Joy said while thinking and recalling the incident, 'I had gone to buy tea to the nearest store. Suddenly, something hit me from back, I bumped on the pole and I fainted right there. When I opened my eyes, I was in a car, I could remember strange faces, they must have taken me to the hospital.'

'But have you seen any truck coming to your side? How can you ignore a big truck and its noise?' Naina asked him to remember and put some light on the incident.

'I was a little drowsy. I had headache at that time as we had a party last night.' Naina understood now that Joy was drunk. He was not completely in his senses; this might be the reason why he could not hear the truck coming from behind, 'Call everybody to the police station, call his friends.'

Rawat asked, 'Yes Ma'am, when do you want them?'
'ASAP!'
Bosky, Rehman, Vandy, Shubh came soon, Jyotika wanted to come with Menka.
Inspector Naina met Shubh first. Shubh helped her to get some basic information. Naina knew their interpersonal relationship affairs. Jealousy might be the reason for these planned accidents.
'You have feelings for Joy, right?' Naina asked looking at Bosky.
'Me and Joy were in Delhi Blind Orphanage, we were together; we are together now too, we are very good friends.'
'But is it true that Joy loves Jyotika and you had a fight over it?' Inspector had all the prior information.
'What an argument! We had fight, but I cannot try to kill someone because of that, we do have fights on many things.' 'Reply, whatever you have been asked to, this is not your music room, you are called in at the police station and it's better for you to remember that. This is my case, no one will go scot free, I am investigating an attempt to murder case.'
Bosky was petrified after she heard the strong words. The musical Rainbow group was offered tea and asked to wait as Inspector Naina had some errands to finish.

After a while, she called Bosky again,
'Who do you think has tried to kill Joy?' Bosky was speechless. She didn't know what to say.
'You claim to be Joy's friend you should know his foe also, didn't that bother you? Haven't you thought about it? If not you should have, as a friend, what do you think?'

Bosky was speechless. Looking straight at her. A whitish look, rough face, hard looking lips, her hair tied in a pony-tail, she might have applied oil on her hair, her police uniform was starched, she was looking as a dangerous lady, she might be around thirty seven. The fan in her cabin was slowly spinning with a mysterious noise, demanding for urgent oil servicing. The staff at police station was careless and was 'least concerned attitude' types.

Jyotika and Menka arrived there, Naina called them immediately and asked Boksy to go out of the cabin. Bosky kept observing the atmosphere in police station. Wooden benches, chairs and tables, books, registers, desktop computers. There was a typical smell of moisture which hinted that these rooms were not properly washed; only cleaned hastily. Moreover, the common people who were sitting in police station were very sad and depressed.

Jyotika and Menka were facing Inspector Naina; Rawat was standing near to assist her,

'There is a conspiracy behind it; love, hate and jealousy has gone far ahead and its killing people. The driver was given contract for killing Joy. He is the same driver who killed Ray; do you have any idea Jyotika who is doing this? What is happening?' Naina asked.

'I have absolutely no clue officer, we are facing really tough time, I am happy that a competent inspector like you is handling the case.' Menka replied.

'Ray is not going to come into our life again . . .' Menka added further, she was sad and devastated, Jyotika was looking at Naina.

'You guys will have to help me or else next target is . . . Tell me who is planning all this? Or else Joy would be targeted again.' After 4 to 5 hours of discussion, interrogation, cross questioning inspector Naina obtained very few information; but she wanted to know who are the people behind their lives, are they connected to some underworld group?

Soon, there was a call from ACP (Assistant Commissioner of Police) for Naina; Rawat said, 'He is asking about the case and has called you immediately' Naina had no option but to leave the police station.

Assistant Commissioner of Police, Khan was waiting for her. 'What is this accident all about having much hype, hue and cry?' ACP Khan questioned.

Joint Assistant Commissioner of Police Raghuvir Gawde was also present in the meeting. Officers in police department normally did not interfere in Naina's case, she had solved many complex cases and so was respected by all for her work. In fifteen years Naina had achieved what many of the police officers might not have thought of! ACP Khan was new; he might have taken in by Joint Police Commissioner Gawde, but why and who wanted to know where the investigation had reached? She was sure about it, now that this case had complicated links might be political.

'This case is beyond accident, I think there is a conspiracy behind it. I am looking for the clue, as of now nothing concrete . . .' Before Naina completed, Gawde took a long breath, 'Khan sir wants you to take your job more seriously; sir was asking me about the MBI, Matunga blast investigation. You are in charge of that case. Do not delay that case because of this accident case.'

'I will pay full attention to that case.' Naina said with determination. ACP smiled, 'Yes, please do so, I have pressure from ministry.'

Naina got up and went outside. Her seniors wanted her not to investigate Joy accident case.

Sheer hard work and honesty never work, she knew it. Right approach and networking in ministry, media, plus striking balance between both is always needed.

She called Abhishek, an established P.R.O in market and leaked the information about the Rainbow group that, the band was in danger and someone wanted to destroy their hard work and identity. The group was growing very fast but somebody was not liking it. Who was that somebody? The reason was not known and police was not paying fullest attention to this case.

Abhishek hyped this story in media. The very next day all news channels and newspapers noticed the news and all the journalists were after the Rainbow group; they had been asked about the case and also who they think might had killed Ray.

"Rainbow music director, Ray was murdered, it wasn't an accident . . ."
Electronic and print media took the story and hyped it.
Jyotika motivated everyone to march.

'This is the time, it would give dedication to Ray's death in real sense, let's march from Churchgate to Gateway of India'. The entire Rainbow group then decided to march with burning candles to grab media's attention and seek public support for the cause.

Menka was also convinced with the idea. That would have really helped them as well as the case, and who so ever was trying to kill them, would have got deterred. They decided to march for justice to the gateway of India. They had gathered a group of supporters with the help of an N.G.O, which again hit the news nationally in electronic and print media. Menka didn't stop there; she had a collection of paintings of Ray which she had been treasuring till date. Abhishek grabbed the opportunity and became a part of their team as an exclusive PR agent of the group. He came with a new idea seeing the collection of paintings of Ray. He suggested for a painting exhibition which was liked by everyone, he took the responsibility to make this exhibition popular.

The painting exhibition was a huge success. Photographs of Ray's paintings were distributed with Rainbow's CDs and appreciated by all.

Social networking sites uploaded Ray's Photos. He became a youth icon overnight. Schools, colleges, educational institutes held debates about Joy's accident and motives behind it.

Charu felt proud of her daughter. Each moment gave her great satisfaction whenever she saw her on TV, or, hitting newspapers' headlines. She didn't have guts to do what her daughter had.

Pratap was silent most of the time and had stopped making her daughter understand. He was waiting and watching silently.

'She will come back once she will realize her mistake, they are using her.' He commented that day, seeing Jyotika's picture in the newspaper.

22

$\mathcal{E}$ach news channel had its own story about it; interviews began, journalists kept on guessing what might have happened in Rainbow team, people started liking Rainbow music. ACP Khan called and asked Gawde about who had leaked this information to media; they knew it was Naina! But the news was already out. Now no one could do anything.

One person who was out of it was Sunny. He was concentrating on work. He was trying to strike a new deal with a foreign collaboration. Koyal was helping him to bring new investments in the company and go international.

Koyal was keeping herself updated about the latest happenings in the Rainbow issue. She was keeping an eye on every coverage released by media, related to this issue. She was confused as who might have contracted to kill Ray? 'Did Sunny do it? No way! It can't be Sunny. His Guruji has blessed him and has assured that soon everything will be alright.'

Pratap Sanyal and Charu were only spectators! Mohan was worried about what will happen next. He kept on meeting Pratap Sanyal. They also tried to sort out the issue, which they knew they could not. Mohan was unhappy with Sanyal and blamed him for letting Jyotika do many things which he didn't approve of. Mohan knew Gujuji would never fail. At the end of the day Jyotika would marry Sunny.

23

The music album proved to be a big hit globally. Menka was very happy. She also appreciated the way media has helped bringing in light Ray's case. Jyotika had special moment with Menka, they became emotional while sharing those moments when Ray was alive and dreamt of this great time.

Rainbow's success was an opportunity relish and enjoy. The show must go on, no matter what difficulty one faces in life . . .

She announced a party to celebrate the success of 'Rainbow,' the dream of her son and the team Rainbow! This was made possible by everyone's hard work.

The party was organized in the music room in the midst of the hill. The evening was ready to melt down into darkness. Everyone left for home, Jyotika and Joy stayed back for a while, having hands entangled, climbing towards the high hill nearby; slowly and steadily, their fingers mingled into each others! Telling the story of their closeness . . .

'Let's go there,' Jyotika said.

'We don't have torch, how will we come back?'

'Why are you thinking of coming back, let's just reach to the destination.'

Both of them started walking, after 20-25 minutes' walk, they reached to the top of the hill. They were unable to see anything. It was all dark, all they knew that they were on the top of the hill; they could only see and feel each other. 'You know the meaning of my name?' Jyotika asked

'Your name means a lot for me', Joy said with smile. 'Jyotika means 'Light'.

'Jyotika' means eyes, light, and vision' Jyotika defines. 'No, it's not the same, light and vision can't be the same.' Joy differed 'I do not know much of the difference but it's not the same Jyotika. Let's ask someone,' Joy said.

'Not a bad idea!'

Jyotika said and came closer to him. They had hardly any distance between their lips. They looked at each other. They could feel each other's breath. Both of them were sure that they wanted to kiss; but there is always a wait before kiss! Kiss is a depiction of love! No one knows why two souls fall in love. There are theories, calculations, researches, claims but for them, till that very moment no one had actually found out a clear formula of love!!

When they decided to mingle themselves, when they started kissing each other, they didn't want to come back, but they had to!!

They had dinner together with everyone and went on the terrace. After an hour Jyotika left for home.

One person who was deeply sad and silently watching them, was Bosky.

Both Joy and Jyotika were unaware of the fact that something shocking was going to happen tomorrow. Early in the morning when Menka called everyone for tea, Bosky didn't get up. She came to know the bad news when the doctor declared Bosky dead. She had taken many sleeping pills which turned into poison to kill her.

Media enjoyed making a new story with creative, innovative headlines:

The dark side of Rainbow - A Dark Rainbow!

Naina knew it! She was right, Love-hate relationship was the reason for every incident taking place. Naina announced while investigations, many more will die in this case.

'What do you think? Why she committed suicide?' Naina asked Rawat.

'I think she was forced to.' Rawat replied when he was asked to apply his mind.

Naina met Joy and Jyotika separately. Jyotika was confident, fearless in her answers, but Joy was afraid! Naina knew the lead is somewhere else. She spent a night thinking about it. She asked for Ray's a murder's forensic reports; she started looking at the case in new light.

24

*T*he forensic report helped Naina to get some clues. Rawat helped her and she decided to investigate families of Jyotika and Sunny. She spoke to everyone except Sunny. The envelopes found in both the accidents had Sunny's company's name printed on them, which was tried to be erased. She knew if she would go in details and arrest anyone, media will hype it again! She wanted to make the moves very carefully. The whole night she was thinking about what can be done! Inspector Naina knew that this case was very important and had great potential, which could benefit her in many ways. She had to choose, 'which way to go, what can be achieved'. She had already grabbed attention by leaking that case with media. It became a case of national importance.

She was from a family where everything was difficult. She struggled hard and had passed out with average marks in her academics. She applied for a post in police force and cleared it. She got a preference in selection procedure because, she belonged to scheduled cast. A poor looking face, body and clothes . . . she was insulted many times during the police training. But her hardworking nature made her learn about this country, called India; where 'poor' are forced to live insulted life only because they are poor.

She climbed the ladder of success, proving everyone wrong who thought that, she had no potential as a police officer. She became a capable senior Inspector in police department. She had great sense to smell a case, which case has potential which doesn't.

She wanted to go back to Pune, the place where she belonged to. She had a daughter who was studying in a local school. She joined police services and got married immediately.

She was divorced after five years of her marriage, her daughter and her old parents were the only family she had. She could not live without them. She always missed her daughter and parents. She wanted transfer to her home town, Pune. This case might had helped her getting transferred.

Naina took her next step, she took warrant and arrested Sunny.

There was a huge cry in public when Sunny was arrested. Journalists, media and everyone were shocked by this great surprising news! Sunny could not believe that he was behind bars. His father Mohan Kumar immediately contacted Swami Guruji. Swami Guruji helped Sunny get out, using his contacts at higher level. He knew some ministers, and superior police officials.

Mohan Kumar and Pratap Sanyal tried their best to see Sunny out on bail as fast as possible. They had a team of top advocates who were being paid like anything to release Sunny.

Naina could not detain him for more than 4-5 hours, he was out on bail, prior to that both Naina and Sunny had conversation in police station.

'I would definitely like to know the evidence against me.' Sunny was curious to know.

'The case is very simple Sunny, one can do anything, harm anyone after having failed in love! You have loved Jyotika since childhood, you are a successful businessman, a winner, but your life is incomplete without Jyotika, so you planned to kill Ray. Jyotika came back in your life and went back to Joy. You were not able to get her after that. Then you decided to kill Joy also and gave money to the same truck driver, but unfortunately this time your plan not only failed but backfired; instead of Joy, the driver who was given money died in that accident.'

Sunny was listening very carefully with a grin on his face. 'It's utter nonsense! This is all your guess! Assumption! There is no truth in it.' He said with smile.

'According to your theory Bosky also comes under suspicion, she also loved Joy.'

'May be, love has that hard emotions, why not? But, unfortunately the evidence goes against you and not against her. She doesn't have money and resources like you,' Naina clarified.

'If you knew that I am known, successful, resourceful, then you shouldn't have made this mistake officer.'

'I do it when I am sure about things.'

'How long do you think you can keep me here?' Sunny asked arrogantly.

'This is not the question; the bigger question is, I have not handcuffed you till now and you should know that, a police officer can do anything in police station, I can beat you like anything.' She said with anger.

Sunny didn't say anything after that, he was scared. The special Magistrate granted his bail in a few hours. He had tears in his eyes when his dad came to meet him. He hugged him tight. He was taken back home, hiding from the media; he was kept in a bigger jail at home, accessible to none. Naina knew it. She knew what she was up to. She had her own plans.

Jyotika was very upset after hearing this news.

Double standard bastard had killed my Ray! She thought.
'How can someone be so cruel?' Joy reacted.

Media was after everyone who was ready to speak about the story of Rainbow, murder, suicide and arrest. Menka, Joy and the entire team was fed up of clarifying the facts. Media was not ready to stop from speculative stories. Each channel had different story to tell.

Naina was making statements in all her interviews that this case had deeply rooted in the mud of money and power and many influential people are involved in it.

'Success and money bring their own problems with them.' She mentioned in one of her interviews. The media hyped her case; her media friends needed story and she knew how and when to leak it.

Joy was hit badly, he was under trauma. Bosky and he were together since Delhi Blind Orphanage, they shared very close moments together. When they were small, they always discussed life in darkness and had always imagined it.

They used to imagine the birds which wake them early in the morning, how they might be looking? The sky, where these birds fly! Their weird, hazy imaginations came true one day. But Bosky forgot that life after getting the vision.

Joy learnt the biggest lesson of life, which was beyond vision, that, someone can even end his life if he doesn't find his love. Love is the most powerful emotion and so the hatred!
She died because she lost her love.
If he was to trust the media story, Sunny killed Ray because he didn't get his love.

He looked at her photograph; she was indeed very beautiful and charming. An orphan blind girl, who had no one except him in this world, had left the world. She couldn't take it; she couldn't tolerate him being Jyotika's boy-friend. Had she done a mistake? Or he had done a mistake? Who's fault was it? Everything was co-related.

Joy wanted light, he got it. His voice was being recognized all over, he was a famous singer. He had Jyotika also! The best girl anyone could dream of getting in life as a girlfriend! He had to be happy, but he was not, why? Why he was feeling guilty about Bosky's death? He had done nothing! He couldn't help it if someone wanted to be loved by someone. He shouldn't take blame on himself making himself sad, why he was sad then? For what? The entire group was sad, everyone was silent . . . including Menka. What to do was the big question! Jyotika was always with them. Jyotika and Joy hardly talked. They knew the reason, they were blaming themselves for Bosky's death.

25

$\mathcal{P}$ratap Sanyal and Mohan Kumar were very upset.

Sanyal and Mohan met senior officials, who were known to Swami Guruji and they offered them huge amount to remove Sunny's name from the case. They got an assurance, but nothing fruitful happened. Swami Guruji then fixed their meeting with home minister Shivraj Kadam. He was a great follower of Swami Guruji.

'Media will create hue unnecessarily, if we remove his name now. He is well caught in media circle, this is not the right time for fetching him out smoothly; but you can always file a defamation case against the lady police officer,' Shivraj Kadam suggested them. But Swami Guruji pressurized him to transfer that lady officer Naina immediately. Home minister knew that Swami Guruji had contacts in central ministry and he could not ignore him.

'You take whatever decision you want, you are home minister and your chunk will be according to your caliber only!' Swami Guruji briefed him on phone.

It meant huge monitory involvement, and Swami Guruji would share that money too.

'Yadav organized a meeting with Pratap Sanyal and Mohan Kumar.' His personal secretary was instructed. Shivraj Kadam had to take decision and take care of these people for sure.

Yadav knew his job very well. Naina was also called immediately.

'What is this? You are troubling a genuine businessman, playing important role for our party, they are our staunch supporters, are you paid any money from opposition for doing all this?' Yadav attacked. He noticed Naina had put on some extra kilos.

'You know, that's not true.' Naina replied looking at the off white starched safari suit of the best brand available in the market. She knew he had suffered two heart attacks and made money in million, kept in an account in Swiss Bank.

'Keep quiet, I will talk to Netaji about your posting, where do you want it?'

'Pune! . . . Transfer with promotion, Shivaji Nagar area, main city.'

'I will recommend, it is possible, but you have to work as we say, do not take any step without our permission,' Yadav warned her.

'As you say,' Naina didn't take a second to think. She looked at him, 'You look fit. Do you still go for morning walk every morning. Take care of your health. Where is your son nowadays?' 'He is studying in London, not doing very well, wasted lot of my money. These children now days . . . What to do!' Yadav became emotional.

'Take care sir.' She knew, she had to maintain balance between image building, media and the case. All cases do not have this kind of potential, where everyone has a chance to serve his purpose. A case like this might have lots of potential, depending upon how the officer was dealing with it. She had to be honest in front of media, grab promotion on the other side and let the case rest. Everyone would have been satisfied that way. A case like this benefits everyone with vested interest. It requires skills to handle it, although it might backfire sometimes.

Yadav called Sanyal immediately after things were fixed.

In around 20 minutes they reached. They saw Naina going out of Yadav's cabin as they entered in the cabin. They exchanged looks. Both the parties had victorious looks on their faces.

Sanyal thought that she was summoned by minister's secretary, for giving a warning to stop all her nonsense. He really deserved to be at the post of a minister's secretary.

Yadav solved everything without a hitch and doubt.

'She was begging! Now she won't do anything. I have threatened her with possible dire consequences.' Yadav made the final remark.

'Thanks Yadavji!' Two of the listed industrialists of the country smiled with relief in front of a broker type typical secretary, who wore off white safari with white shoes and was a chain smoker, a packet of cigarette was kept on the table with an expensive lighter on the top.

'Thanks? For what? You both are respected rich men, and who is she? A fucking bitch! She will be transferred to some place soon. You will read it very soon. How dare she put your son in custody! Do not worry at all! Just see now! And you tell me anything, I can do it for you. What would you like to have, tea, coffee?' They smiled. They knew money has this power which can buy people like him.

'Where do you want the money?' Sanyal was quick.

'Send cash to the same courier company. Ghanshyam Das, He will come to your office to collect parcel.'

Smart moves were made by these people, who run the country called India, top businessmen and politicians are genius in money transactions. The money transaction was taking place through a courier company; no one could have doubted that!

SwamiGuruji was called by had gifted a huge amount of money, as because of him the case reached to a positive end.

Koyal was the only person, who was clueless about what was happening. Koyal was completely confused. She loved a person, left everything for him, left a booming career in modeling and helped him in his business by bringing in lots of investments.

Today, he was being accused of killing someone.

Koyal left home when she was very young. She came to Mumbai from Kolkata to become an actress. She started with modeling, met dozens of designers in the industry, traveled all over the world and earned a lot of money at a very young age. She met Sunny in Frankfurt airport waiting for a plane; she wanted to talk to someone for some time as she was feeling low.

'Hi, can I borrow your pen for a while?' Koyal began the talk.

'Ya, sure.'

Koyal returned the pen after working on puzzles in the newspaper.

'Are you a model?' Sunny looked at her, she was tall, fair and sexy.

'Ya, signing a film soon.'

'And you?' The conversation began to end nowhere. They became friends and stayed in touch for a long time. Koyal's film began, ended as a flop. Her uncle visited Mumbai and showed interest in investing lots of money in film business. Koyal took him to Sunny rather than taking him to a film producer.

She knew uncle wanted a profitable business and that was definitely not films.

Koyal began to work as a business partner as uncle had no time to look after that. She began to like Sunny and thought that, she might have a settled life with him. She was fed up with unsuccessful films, it was a tough career choice, few people become successful and many lived unemployed.

She learnt business, uncle taught her the gimmicks of business. She was fast and interested in it also! Sooner she came to know that business is all about making deals, keeping organization and employees updated with new policies. Company makes profit only if tie-ups are safe.

Uncle, her only family member demised one day. She put herself into business completely.

She fell in love with Sunny didn't know what the truth of the moment is? Who killed Ray? And who tried to kill Joy? Why sunny had no compassion towards her love? Was Sunny a right person? She got a call from Sunny.

'Hi Koyal, are you at home?'

'Yes, I am. What happened? Where are you now?'

'I am reaching there, at your flat in some time. 9 O'clock at night, Sunny drove down to Koyal's flat evading media.

Sunny arrived at Koyal's flat after half an hour. Koyal was disturbed to see Sunny at her home. He hugged Koyal. But she was hesitant; she wanted to know more about the case. She was worried, not interested in hugging him. She was thinking all those hours and days about Sunny; what kind of person he was? Could he kill someone? Whatever it was but he was facing murder charges. Anything can happen in love, but Sunny killing someone, seemed impossible.

Newspapers were full of stories about this case. But wasn't it right to support him? This was the time when he needed her support and by doing that she might have got closer to him, Koyal thought this was a chance, golden chance, she shouldn't miss that. 'I need a glass of water,' Sunny sat on the sofa and asked her to bring some water, she followed the same. She brought a glass of water. 'What is happening Sunny? Why everyone has gone against you? I am not able to understand all this.'

'Life is full of challenges, sometimes you have to search through to find the truth. Swami Guruji always says that destiny can't be changed. That was my destiny to go to jail, but with the grace of Swami Guruji I was out in only a few hours.'
'Swami Guruji said destiny can't be changed, so how can he change your destiny? Is he God?' Koyal was fed up listening this Swami crap for long.
'We are very small to question Swami Guruji. Accept whatever he says.
Do whatever he asks you to do. That is his first teaching.' Sunny told her with pride.
'I was with you, I am, and will be with you, always.' Koyal said without any doubt and question.

Sunny looked at her, she was the one who always supported him in every situation.
Sunny got up and hugged her tight; very tight, both of them felt for each other. Sunny kissed on the back of her neck, she felt the sensation. The blood ran fast through her veins and led to further act.

A great sexual welcome offer, to enter in the world of love, she waited for long time. She also kissed on his neck, she was taller too, a perfect match!

Sunny brought her face in front of his face and kissed; kissed her lips slowly, she felt the shiver. This was time to think of nothing. Both of them were engrossed in making love, stole moments from time . . .

Koyal rapped white bedsheet and moved to the balcony nudging her head to spread her hair on shining naked shoulders. Her bosoms shook inside the white bedsheet, it was a show off to show her fantastic body in shape which can invite and lure anyone to touch. Sunny pulled the bedsheet to see her completely naked. He did see.
She fell in his clutch on his lap.
She smiled.

'So?' . . .
'So?' . . .

These 'so' were very different from those which they had interacted millions times. These were mysterious in nature, without any mystery hidden. Sunny held her tightly in his arms to kiss her. Koyal let her body leave at his disposal.

She went and made black coffee for two of them to enjoy.

She finished the coffee and lied down on the same bed where Sunny was lost in his thoughts. He smiled looking at her. She was an amazing beauty, fair skin, long legs, spotless beauty, shining like hot sun; a perfect body, one could imagine before going to bed every night.

Koyal sat beside him like an obedient kid. She felt power of Sunny had entered in herself. She felt that she was the owner of the same powerful persona.

He asked something for eating.
Koyal wasted no time to order food.

'So?' Sunny smiled.
'So . . .' Koyal smiled too.

'Shall I ask you something?' Koyal looked into his eyes.
'Go ahead sweetheart.'

'What is all this going on, why they are against you?'

'Papa and uncle have settled the case, Guruji knows the minister, I am innocent, time will prove.' He took a pause, took her hand into his hands and said with emotions.

'I am not here for that, I am here to say,' he took a pause, looked into her eyes

'I love you. Will you marry me?' Koyal couldn't believe it. The time stopped for her.

Sunny was proposing her for marriage.

That was the moment he made a decision. He felt happy and joyful and that's it!! What else one needs in life?

26

*I*n the morning at around 10 O'clock Naina called up Rawat and discussed the case again. Rawat disclosed a new finding that a man called Bhagat was involved in it. He was an old worker, loyal to Jyotika's dad. Bhagat had been seen meeting the truck driver's family after the death of a driver. That was indeed a strong piece of evidence.

Naina wanted to know who was the culprit, so that she could defend herself in the future if anything would go against her. Both of them immediately rushed to the driver's family.

Her transfer order could have come at any moment. Before anything new could happen she wanted to solve the case. Bhagat was a freelancer. He worked as a spy for corporate companies and used to provide information against those who used duplicate products of companies.

Rawat was right; Bhagat was the key person in this case. Bhagat worked for Jyotika's dad's company too. Later, they came to know that he was also pitching work for Sunny. He needed money, a man was known as a womanizer, gambler and working as agent for a company getting their work done. Bhagat was friendly with all types of people. A man like him remained loyal to all these industrialists. He had the potential! Naina couldn't understand; the case was a real puzzle. There was a girl who was also involved actively, who was that girl? Was somebody trying to use this girl or was this girl a pivotal for incident? The entire day passed.

Naina again viewed the CCTV camera footage which they had got from the jewelry shop when Ray died; but Joy's accident was not covered by CC TV camera footage. Rawat disclosed that there was some connection between this girl and Bhagat. Rawat had monitored Bhagat's activities and enquired in the vicinity where Bhagat lived, about what he does and everything. Bhagat was a controversial guy. Both Naina and Rawat checked his background, they tapped his phone conversations.

Tapping phone conversation was an eye opener for the case.

Bhagat was in constant touch with Pratap Sanyal and Mohan Kumar.

The phone records showed a girl, whose cell was found switched off and untraceable. Naina tried calling the number but was in vain.

It was a waste of time. There was a call from minister's residence, might be of Yadav. She ignored the call for time being. Yadav's man arrived with the transfer letter in hand. Monkar, a man who was close to Yadav.

'Madam, I had gone to your residence, you were not there. Sir had asked me to deliver this order as soon as possible.' 'Hmm! Have a sit. Do you want some tea?' Naina took the letter. Monkar left immediately. He made a call to Yadav before leaving.

Rawat was zapped! She had been transferred. Rawat was close to her. He didn't know who was replacing Naina? What kind of person would he be? Rawat helped her pack her stuff. She left for Pune. She didn't know what was going to happen with the case. She had done whatever she could. Police job serves the one who has vested interests. One has to understand lobby, work in lobby and work for the lobby! Lobby helps at the end of the day. She had nothing to do with this case. She knew that the truth will be known to few. For everyone else it will be a mystery.

27

Kamal Narayan, a minister's obedient police officer was the new man in the game.

'Clean the mess created by that bitch. These women! They do not fit in the police job. They are good for nothing. Now she has been transferred. Sanyal, Mohan and his son Sunny should come clean. Close the case as soon as possible. And let me know the truth. I should be reported on daily basis.' Narayan was instructed clearly by the Homeminister of state. Rawat briefed him the entire case.

Sunny was the one person, who seemed not to be involved in any illegal act. As Narayan checked all his previous records, not a single call was fishy. All calls were short and he hardly had made any call to anyone, he either had received calls or they had ended as missed calls. They found nothing against him, Sunny was innocent. Inspector Narayan realized that Sunny was made a scapegoat. Was it a mistake or a deliberate act?

Narayan met the minister next day, and reported him that, prima facie it looked like Sunny was innocent. Naina had some motives behind arresting Sunny. She suddenly arrested him so that, case could be hyped and pressure could be created; and she achieved it by leaking it in media. Narayan was a competent official, he understood the metrics behind her moves.

'Take media in favor, you must be knowing people in media.'

'Yes, I do. I have many friends in media.'

'Give him a clean chit; call a press conference, immediately,' Yadav instructed him.

Home Minister Kadam and his secretary told Sanyal that soon things would be in their favor. He was loyal. He would take money to produce result, their party was known for that. The media was called and informed about the innocence of Sunny.

'Why did he get arrested then, if he was innocent and who is the killer?' Asked, one of the journalists.

'I am new officer here; the previous officer has been transferred as you all know. The truth will be out soon, after thorough investigation. All we know at this moment is that, Sunny has been victimized and has been accused wrongly.'

'What is the hurry? Till now the investigation is also incomplete.' Another journalist supported Naina's act. 'The announcement was not about Sunny but about me taking over the case; but at the same time I also came to know from my sources that Sunny is innocent.'

Sunny was relieved. He conveyed his decision about marriage to his parents that, he was going to marry Koyal. Everyone took a sigh of relief. They thought, 'It's good if they are getting settled.

'Jyotika anyways didn't wish to marry Sunny. So it's great in fact!' Mohan thought so.

Narayan began his investigation as he had to report back to his bosses to prove his loyalty.

'Bhagat was the one who had actually done that, and Pratap Sanyal and Mohan Kumar are also involved. The only mystery of the case is a girl's number; the girl who was actively involved in the entire scenario. She was in constant touch with Bhagat. We have her number, by tomorrow morning her name will be revealed.' Rawat explained the case to Narayan, his new boss! He explained further, 'the girl who was in touch with Bhagat and met him many times outside his home was half blind.'

'What do you mean by half blind?'

'She could see only with one eye.'

'Who is this girl who is half blind and who was influencing Bhagat? The puzzle is still unsolved, why that girl was taking interest in Bhagat? Pratap Sanyal and Mohan Kumar's involvement can be understood, but this girl's involvement is a big question mark!' Narayan was curious.

28

Rawat and Narayan tracked the address of the mobile phone available with the mobile company. It was none other than Bosky's mobile number. The musical group got another shocking news. But Bosky was already dead. The mystery of Bosky's cell number remained unsolved.

Bhagat's arrest was mandatory. Bhagat was tracked and arrested immediately. Narayan had strong network of people who helped him to track the location of Bhagat.

Narayan wanted all the information from Bhagat.
'Your arrest is unofficial till this moment.' Narayan told him coldly, 'But it can be turned into an official arrest, if you do not tell me the truth.'
Bhagat knew that there was no way out.
'I will tell everything sir, will you let me go then?'
'Are you trying to dictate terms on me?' Narayan was angry this time.
'Tell me the truth first, I will see what I can do for you, but only when I will know the complete truth. A lie will drive you behind the bars for whole life or may lead to death sentence. Choice is yours.' Narayan warned him!
Bhagat knew, if someone could save him, it was officer Narayan and he decided not to make him angry, rather help him with the truth so that he would consider releasing him from the unofficial arrest.

Bhagat revealed everything.

It was shocking a information. The first accident was plotted by Mohan Kumar and Pratap Sanyal to kill Ray because they did not want Jyotika to marry Ray. They had appointed him for the job and he hired driver Sunil who used to do this kind of work for years.

The second revelation was more amusing! Bosky plotted to kill Joy and the second contract was given by Bosky to him and he hired Sunil again; but unfortunately Sunil died in that act. Bhagat further explained that, Bosky was horrified after visiting the police station. Bosky had stolen jewelry from Menka's safe, sold it and gave it to Bhagat to kill Joy.

Bosky was burning with jealousy every moment. Her life had become hell. She tried all possible means to control her emotions. She could not understand whether it was love or hate which had overpowered her. She began to go to temples to have peace of mind. She used to sit for hours alone in the temple. She found out an old couple who were blind and used to come there and sing for hours. She started enjoying their company.

One night Bosky was looking for a taxi while coming from Mahalaxmi temple. Bhagat, suddenly stopped his car and offered her lift. He said he knew her, he further claimed that, in fact he knew entire the Rainbow group including Jyotika. Bosky was not willing to accompany a stranger, but she thought God might be leading her to some hope. Her superstitions took a wrong turn. Bhagat's narration was deadly.

'So, do you visit this temple often?' Bhagat.

'Yes, every Monday evening; and I wait till late night, till the temple closes.'

'You come alone?'

'Ya . . .Menka had come once for few minutes, after that she went back.' Bhagat described meeting with Bosky, which was purely coincidental; Bosky was sad and shared everything during the tiresome traffic from Mahalaxmi to Bandra.

'Why are you unhappy?'

'I don't know, but I can't see Joy and Jyotika together.'

'Hmm what if one of them dies . . .' Bhagat initiated.

'Sorry?' She was shocked for a moment.

'In the accident, like Ray died.' She was shocked about where the conversation was leading?

'Ray has been killed by someone? It wasn't an accident?' She decided to step out of the car.

'I want to leave, please stop the car.'

'I stopped the car and gave my card to her if she required to call me.'

'She called you later, right?' Narayan asked.

'She called me after two weeks and met me when she was determined to do something.

'We met at Bandstand, during the peak hours of the day.' Bhagat spoke after having a deep breath.

'And what did she say when she met you?'

'She said, she was disturbed and couldn't sleep or work or unable to do anything; All the time she was thinking of one thing, that was Jyotika and Joy being together! I was astonished that she didn't want to kill Jyotika but Joy. She wanted Jyotika to be alive and suffer. She was very much upset with both of them. She was burning from inside!'

She hated him, and didn't want to forgive as he ditched her.

'I wanted five lakhs for that. Bosky sold all her jewelry and also she stole jewelry from Menka's safe, she had some savings too which she gave me.

I paid fifty thousand to the driver in the same envelope, which he had taken from a scrap shop. I had no idea that the envelope had the name of Sunny's company. Incidentally, the driver died and the money did not reach the driver's family. I pressurized Bosky for more money. Bosky was petrified after meeting Naina.'

'You took five lakhs from her and paid fifty thousand to the driver.' Narayan clarified.

'Yes sir, in this kind of work we get this kind of money sir.' Bhagat was scared while saying that. He wanted Narayan to trust him.

'Hmm!' Narayan said, 'Hope whatever you said has truth in it.'

'Sir, this is the truth; nothing but the truth.'

'Bosky did sleep with you, didn't she? You pressurized her for money and She . . .' Narayan insisted.

His mind was running with 100 miles speed to know things.

'I am asking something . . .'

'No sir, who said that?'

'When she had nothing to give, what did she do?'

'Sir trust me that hadn't happen. I wanted money for Sunil's family. She wasn't able to give that money. She was very sad, I pity her.' Narayan guessed that in this kind of situation such things happen.

But Bhagat was not ready to accept that.

Narayan arrived at minister's residence and reported everything and asked what was to be done with Bhagat who was still in his custody.

'Keep him for some more days without showing official arrest.' Home Minister of the State ordered his loyal inspector. The minister wanted to negotiate with Sanyal and Mohan. Yadav called them again, for an urgent meeting.

The meeting was held in Lonavala. The minister's chopper arrived at his bungalow, late night. Sanyal and Kumar were waiting for him since one hour.

'It's a complicated case. Bhagat is in custody. He has vomited everything.' Yadav explained, while Minister Kadam was posing with a heroic and thoughtful face.

'Do something sir, please find a way out; whatever it may take, media shouldn't know about it.'

'We will expose before media about that girl . . .what's her name . . . ? Ya, Bosky!' He remembered the name.

'Rest will be left on media to do the guesswork. The media will take Bosky's story because she is the sensation today.' 'What about Bhagat?' Pratap Sanyal was worried.

'Bhagat is in our custody, has been arrested already,' Yadav again explained the situation.

'Bhagat is our man, he can open his mouth in future.' Mohan Kumar showed the concern.

'I have a suggestion; you take his bail. He will be obliged. And then he will work as your man in future also. Killing him may cause problems. This is a hot story for media today; you know how deadly these media dogs are these days!'

'Hmm, this is a good idea.' Sanyal looked satisfied.

'We will ask inspector to make a weak case against him.' There was silence for some time. The orderly entered with ice and bottles. The minister hinted him to stop for some time and to wait outside till the final deal is done. 'This will cost you a reasonable amount which will reach to you soon. And also this time the money will be transferred to Swiss bank.'

'We are ready for that, that's not a big deal.' They knew that it was an opportunity.

They would have a contract from the same ministry and could make lots of money, they could double the amount which they were investing.

The orderly then was called. He organized the table and left the room. Two beautiful models, who were waiting for a long time, entered the room with a smile and began to serve. The champagne bottles were opened with typical sound and shared by them.

Next day, Yadav called Narayan to brief him about the orders.

'Make the arrest official, Bhagat will get bail soon. You can negotiate your price with either Bhagat or Sanyal. Arrange for statements with the media, take full advantage of solving this case, and close the case, shut the files,' Yadav briefed.

Narayan was a tough negotiator, he got good amount from Bhagat as well as Sanyal and Mohan. Rawat was happy too, he knew that Narayan sir was better than Naina, any day, any time.

A good police case benefits everyone. Naina got posting of her choice, minister got lots of money, Sanyal won the case after killing someone, without even going to court, Narayan got publicity in media and once again proved himself as a capable officer.

The news spread all over. It was a heated press conference.

'So, did Bosky kill Ray too?' The question answer session began.

'Do not get confused. Bosky gave contract to the driver, she herself didn't kill anyone.' Narayan clarified.

'What's the role of Bhagat then?'

'We need Bhagat for many other cases; he is also involved in this case indirectly. He has been arrested as he is the only live witness we have, rest everyone is dead'.

'What is role of Naina? Why has she been transferred?'

'I will only speak about my job and not about others.' Smart officer Narayan clarified.

Joy was shocked! He was the one, who was most affected by knowing the truth. He became very quiet.

'For us everything is visible in half, we live as incomplete. We do not know anything, we see letters but can't read, without reading we can't have knowledge, without knowledge we can't be like others . . .' He reminisced Bosky saying this, when she got vision. She lost her life after having vision. New things became unimportant, everything lost its charm. Happiness disappeared like floss of the soap! Joy started aspiring for knowing about what is life. He started craving for it, just like someone dreamt of buying an expensive car, which he knew he would never imagine buying . . .Mohan Kumar and Pratap Sanyal decided to celebrate. They decided to party at Mohan's. It was a big success for them. When they were drinking champagne, Sunny heard their conversation, which he was not supposed to.

He was zapped with the thoughts.

'What will happen when Jyotika will come to know about it? How would she react to all these issues? There is a point in life where she must understand things she can change; and things she can't change!' He made himself understand that, these things are beyond change so let them be as they were. He heard noises from the living room. He found Pratap and Mohan are fighting loudly.

'Let's then disassociate! We will not work or do business together,' Sanyal said and left.

Sunny didn't stop him. They were in their senses in fact!
'They only talk sensible when they are drunk!'

Generally, all major decisions are taken when a regular drunkard is drunk. Pratap left to not to come back again. Guruji was not happy with it, he tried to mediate.

Home Minister had different views on that, when Yadav informed him about their serious fight and differences.
'Let both of them be our men; and we will deal with them separately. We will create a competition and make them prove who is more loyal.' Minister Kadam proved why he was Home Minister and has Yadav as his

secretary, making this statement. Yadav smiled and heartily appreciated him. Mohan Kumar disassociated with Sanyal finally, they threatened each other about going to Court. Sunny's marriage with Koyal was announced immediately after the incident. Sunny's marriage was the news of the city. It was a pompous marriage. It was indeed a special and enormous event. The relationship was broken so much that Sanyals didn't even attend the marriage, neither were invited for the marriage.

29

*C*haru became a silent spectator.

She found Pratap had become bitter, unconcerned and absent minded.

"See what can be done, . . . I am ok with it, let's see, what did you say? Fire him if anyone is not in time, change the staff, recruit new people, I don't care, don't call me . . ."

Charu was observing him quietly. He had become indifferent to his business and personal life as well. She knew he was angry at himself. He wanted to control things but he could not, so was frustrated because of helplessness.

She knew she could do nothing.

Jyotika was least concerned about these happenings around her. She was busy in her own world. Music, interviews, media, promotion, Bosky tragedy, there were lot of things to face. She didn't have time to think, who was getting married to whom?

'We can tie up with an international company taking interest to buy our rights.' Manoj knew one Magan Bhai, an agent who had links.

'We should meet this guy.'

Jyotika looked at Menka to call the shots on that.

'No harm in meeting him, ask him to organize a meeting with music company.' Magan Bhai was influential. He organized the meeting within next two hours. Jyotika and Menka went for the meeting.

'We are interested, since people have liked your music, but I see promotion and marketing is not as good as expected, we will do it together and share profit.'

'Would there be any payment upfront?' Menka knew little bit of business.

Yes . . . why don't you sell the entire rights to us?' The offer was made by CEO of Lemon Rocks.

'Sarayu music, is known globally, we have our network. I will help promoting you across the world, provided we hold the entire electronic copyright.'

The deal was struck after long negotiations. The Sarayu music will be the sole copyright holder and will pay 40 million US dollars plus the company will bear all promotion expenses of international shows and events.

Pratap couldn't believe it, 40 million US dollars!

'If, Ray had been alive, he would have been his son-in-law.

Rich and famous, cute looking guy, Jyotika paired very well with him.

What a blunder!' Mohan influenced him for this heinous crime, to kill an innocent boy! He shouldn't have listened to him. He repented.

'This all happened because of Jyotika. We should be proud of her.'

'I am proud of her!' He said and went inside the room. Charu went to meet Menka.

Menka was calm. She welcomed her and offered snacks and coffee.

'Everyone has to die, Ray has made his name even after death. He got his due. He has become immortal' Menka was composed. 'I miss Bosky more than Ray, I pray for her, may her restless soul rest in peace'.

'I have come here to congratulate you for your success! When are you going for the global promotion?'

'Next week.'

The Rainbow musical band left for world tour.

Pratap slapped the driver one day when he dashed the car.

'Get off from the car!' He fired him after slapping him tight.

That night he was drunk when he reached home driving his car.

'What's wrong?' He cried, hugging Charu like a kid.

'I don't know what is happening in my life please don't leave me.'
Charu was shocked seeing him like this.

Jyotika was the main boss of the musical band as far as the decision
making was concerned. London, was their first desired destination.

Everything was new for Joy, the flights, people, everything! He always
had fear while approaching and looking at new things and observing the
details.

He was looking at the glittering airports and people were looking
at him that, why this young man was looking at things with so much
of curiosity. The flight took off; he was flying with Jyotika in the sky,
thinking that it was all dream!
'Pinch me, am I dreaming?' Joy looked outside from the window.
'Pinch me too Joy! I have stopped dreaming after Ray has left us. I
thought,
I would never be happy again, but I am, today!' Jyotika said with
happiness.

They reached London. Joy felt the cold breeze penetrating through
his bones. He saw white people with bright skin everywhere. Dust free
air, pollutionfree atmosphere, the popular capital of London was awesome
and fascinating.

Left hand drive, fast moving cars, system completely organized. Joy
felt everything was big and rich and stupendous. Huge metro, trains
moving one above the other, competing with the speed of wind. No soil,
concrete everywhere. A combination of ancient and modern architecture,
London was completely fascinating for him.

Subconscious mind of Joy knew that, he was at a place which rules
the world.

Lemon Rocks had already appointed an event manager at London,
who had organized everything. They went for practice, so that they
wouldn't be nervous at the time of performance.

Joy was little uncomfortable and confused about the show and his singing. He wasn't very sure about his performance.

He vomited twice. He couldn't take the anxiety.
He was a little nervous about things.

The show was anchored by Mark Robin. He had lots of skills to make the audience glued to their seats. Mark had Indian origin, whose ancestors then settled in London long time back, when British were ruling India.

His father was in British army. He had taught, motivated and trained his son about how to evade stage fear. The main audience was of Asian origin; they were from Pakistan, India, Bangladesh, Gulf countries, Malaysia and many other countries. Some of them were special guests invited from London local administrators, who left the show soon after it began.

The audience liked the show. The feed back came from event manager, Patrick Walls 'not bad, better luck next time.' Patrick Walls suggested them to be more confident and free while performing.

Mark threw a party for the first show. Mark had a huge bungalow. The party began with liquor and snacks. Joy noticed two things, the snacks and food had lot of non-vegetarian items in it; and another thing he did notice that, Mark was trying to impress Jyotika.

He was always around her, Jyotika had idea of English music. She had world famous singers' CDs, like Celine Dion, Bryan Adams, Michael Jackson, Madona, Rhydian . . . in her car, which Joy had tried to understand many times but could not. Joy felt lonely, everyone was familiar with that kind of music and Jyotika was also taken away by Mark for dance; she didn't say 'no' to Mark.

For everyone else there was nothing wrong in that, anyway. Vandy and Rehman were dancing with many British friends of Mark. Joy felt sad and ignored; so he began to drink, unknown with the fact that these foreign brands of liquor are far stronger than Indian brands, he lost control after some time and was not able to see or understand where he was going, what he was doing.

He created a scene in the party, which was embarrassing for his group. Menka then took care of him.

'Has he never had drinks? Or is having it for the first time?' Mark asked seeing all that.

'No, he is not; and he will be fine!' Jyotika felt insulted and ignored the answer. Joy had gone completely out of control, he urinated in his pants at the end; and that was the height. The party ended after that.

30

*J*oy was taken to his room. Jyotika personally made sure that he takes bath. He was given a glass of fresh lime. Joy had a sound sleep after that.

Joy got up late, around 11 am in the morning. He had headache. He recalled everything, last night was tough; he had enough, enough of everything, his actions, drinks, stupidity, embarrassment everything! He thought of Jyotika and Mark and the party. Horrible, what was he going to do? And the bigger question was what Jyotika would do? Last night he had acted crazy, like a man without clothes! Naked! Exposed himself that he could't drink; that, he didn't belong to an elite class, but was a backward half blind! The thoughts were killing him. He went to get fresh, took bath and came out to see his friends. Rehman met him first.

'What's wrong?'
'Nothing, last night was horrible man, sorry for that.'
'You embarrassed us a lot. Everyone was . . . Forget it you must be fine now, how are you feeling now? Do not drink next time.' Rehman warned him politely.
'I do not know what happened? How it happened? I had drunk many times before, it never happened before?'
'That brand was expensive and strong. You always had lighter brands, remember?'

'Hmm.' Joy agreed.

'Where is Jyotika?' Joy didn't see her around.

'She had gone with Mark. We have our next show in Yorkshire. Mark is also coming with us. Jyotika is planning to take him for the entire world tour. He has been assigned for that'. Joy didn't like to hear that, but he heard that. He didn't like that guy, Mark, who claimed to be rich and smart.

'Catty eyes he has! These are very dangerous creatures, Jyotika doesn't know this,' he thought.

Mark and Jyotika came little late in the evening. Joy had had his lunch and made few calls to Jyotika which she didn't pick. Joy was very upset.

Jyotika was still talking to Mark in the lobby. Joy didn't say anything to her, he decided to be in his room. Jyotika came in after almost an hour. He began to watch a film on TV . . .

'What's wrong Joy? You saw me in the lobby and came back to your room. Last night was so embarrassing, why did you drink if you can't digest? There should be a limit of drinking. You know, you were guest to someone's house and you peed in your pants.' Jyotika was never like that, never!

For the first time she was saying something like that, perhaps showing her real color.

Joy was silent; emotionally broken by the time. Tears rolled on his cheeks. Jyotika didn't see that, she was busy in complaining.

Joy kept on weeping silently. The moment Jyotika saw him crying she stopped suddenly. She didn't know what to do?

'Why was he crying? Such an emotional fool! Can't even understand what had he done?' She went close to him and hugged him. Need of the day! She knew she loved him.

Joy was like a child. Didn't say anything and kept on crying. This time, more loudly, when she hugged him, he was sitting on bed and crying. Innocent guy! Never faced this kind of situation in his entire life.

'I am sorry,' his broken voice made Jyotika melt with sympathy.

'I will never drink in life again, promise,' asssured Joy.

Jyotika smiled and kissed him.

'I didn't say that, but if you say so, do not forget your promise good boy.' Jyotika knew he wouldn't touch liquor again. He was a strong man. Sometimes in life you have to be strong when these kind of situations occur. She had no word to say, when Joy peed in his pants, everyone was watching him and her, she felt like she had actually did that.

Next destination was Yorkshire. The show was good; Mark got more appreciation. His funny jokes and stage appearance was mind blowing, everyone liked that. Joy was little down and couldn't perform well this time.

The team visited Europe, then Paris, Berlin, Frankfurt Stuttgart, Geneva and finally they landed at Los Angeles. Joy noticed that Jyotika was getting closer to him. Menka was always with him, explaining the richness of these places and being an Indian and Asian how we are behind.

These places were great. Joy found out a lot of difference in Indian cities and foreign states. No city in India can be compared with these world class places, with clean air, cool atmosphere, care and respect for human life, advanced technology.

'They must have worked hard to make their cities great,' he thought.

Los Angeles was the last destination. They were supposed to go back after that, with a hope that they will come back again to cover more cities. Joy was with Menka. Menka was guiding him how to concentrate on singing. She was the only one who appreciated, encouraged Joy a lot. She was the best company. He tried his best to perform as singer, but he noticed, his love was no more his love. Jyotika's priority had changed. Her choice had changed. He found Jyotika had changed. Joy knew, he had lost Jyotika. Joy was alone and devastated by the time. Life had taken a new turn now, Jyotika and Mark were always together. Joy went on the sea shore; he saw Jyotika and Mark standing and talking there already. He turned to go back. Jyotika saw him, she followed and stopped him.

'Why are you going back Joy? Come, see and feel the sea breeze. It's cold, but soothing. See it's so clean. Our beaches in Mumbai are so dirty, see these people, how they keep their things clean. Come join us.' Joy stopped for a while looked at her and smiled.

'You are right, this place is very clean and so the people'. Joy said and looked at Mark. Mark left immediately saying, 'I have something to finish, you guys please continue.' Mark left them alone, so that they can finish their talk and he knew that there were many unfinished topics, they had to finish.

Jyotika didn't say anything she wanted him to leave them alone this time. The waves were making playful sounds. Joy began, 'I see you are getting very close to Mark.'

'He is a friend, a close friend. He helped us making these shows successful, don't you think so? He deserves to be our friend.'

'He is being paid for that.'

'Ya, but everyone is being paid for his work Joy, you too.'

'Are you comparing me with Mark? Mark and me are same for you?' Joy objected.

'Professionally yes, you both are the same'.

'And personally? How close is Mark now?'

'Do not say that Joy, do not even think of that. I love you, but it doesn't mean I can't be friends with anyone. Mark is just a friend, I love you.'

'I do not know who do you love, I think you love only yourself.'

Joy said and left.

Jyotika was standing alone besides the sea in America, thinking that she might have lost her love. He was so mean, how could he think this way. Mark had helped them to get all that business. They had actually made lots of profits, earning Dollars and Euros because of Mark's business skills. He was so resourceful, he cracked the deal with sponsors.

Joy is jealous, may be. He will be okay soon. He doesn't understand business. He should know that life needs money. If we have to make another album and need to promote it, then we need money. Creativity is useless without money. Ray was very talented but did he make any musical album successful? He went without making it. Joy doesn't know the truth of the life. She didn't want any money. The money she had earned would have helped her for making Music Company, buying a place for the recording studio. She was planning for that.

The water of the sea was shining, she noticed that it had blue effect, which was turning dark.

She came to her room and saw Menka. She had hardly any talk during the tour with Menka. Actually she was all the time with Mark, she spent the maximum time with him. Menka smiled, 'Where are you beautiful, no time for me?' That was everyone's complaint, She felt like talking to Menka.

'Who says that? I am not a busy person at all. I am just trying to organize everything for the show. This for me is also a new experience all together, very tiresome and hectic. These events are time killing. Mark is the only person who has experience. You know he told me how to organize everything. He helped me a lot. He is really a kind hand in our group. See how he manages the stage with confidence, audience enjoy his presence.' Jyotika justified.

'Mark Robin is not a singer sweetie; he is there for a few moments! People come here to hear and see Rainbow group singing for them! These songs are very melodious and attention grabbing. Haven't you read the media review? They praise the team and the songs. They have performed for the first time and they performed like professionals. A shadow represents the body of the object it belongs to, and do not get confused with it. Music is a difficult art which comes from practice and dedication. They have worked hard on it.' Menka tried to make her point understand her. She had seen the world.

Jyotika wasn't convinced. But she could not ignore it either. She didn't want to say anything which might have hurt her. She was like her mom. She was a great help during the tour. Jyotika felt very clearly that everyone is against Mark, but why? Joy, she could understand that Joy was jealous; he was in love with her, but Menka? What was wrong with her? Calling him a shadow, a person who represented these people, he has no entity? What rubbish! She thought, Menka was from last generation, so she couldn't understand those things.

It was time to go. Mark gifted her golden key ring at the airport. They hugged each other. Jyotika had tears in her eyes, they came just like that. How? Why? Everyone noticed that. Jyotika knew they will think otherwise, but she loved Joy; in this life Joy was the one and only; who else could have take his place in her heart.

31

*I*ndia was perceived hot and dirty while coming back from abroad. India has two prime things, heat and dust, Joy began to hate his homeland.

'After so many years of independence there is no progress at all! What kind of nation is this? Where was I born? Why did he born in this part of the world? Why in Asian continent? He was asking questions to himself.'

He thought, he lived in a corrupt country, where most of the politicians were shameless criminals facing serious charges. There was no city in India which was of international standard. None! He lived in Mumbai, but that too he was not proud of. The city was full of dirt, slum, and poverty.

Why his country was a poor one?

He was born blind, lived in orphanage without proper meals.

How was he born? Who were his parents? How did he come to orphanage? Was he born as an illegitimate child?

The curiosity sucked his mind whenever he thought about it. It pained him many a times that he couldn't know his parents' identity. But, didn't he get love from his friends?

He was saddened with pain during recent world tour. He was looking out from the window of the Frankfurt university, the huge campus, made with great skills. Menka was taking him to show the university.

'Didn't you get love form your friends?' Asked Menka
'I did.' He replied.
'Am I not your mother?'
Joy looked at her. She hugged him.
'You are my mom.' He cried like a kid.

At Frankfurt, he was freezing with cold. He looked outside the window the entire area was white, covered with snow.
It looked calm. Quiet.
He did have a life he could be proud of.

'Ok, reply my question now.'
'Where did those children come from who has parents, where did those parents come from?'
'I didn't understand your question?'
'Where would anyone go after death, after life, and where were they before life.' Joy asked.
'How would one know? If you really wanna search anything, search this question and get the answer, let me know also when you know the answer.

Ice wasn't melting outside but inside also, Joy was curious, looking at the snow, and the crane which was trying to clear it.

Menka enlightened him about a new journey.
Only a mother could have done that he knew.

Pratap hugged Jyotika and cried like an innocent boy, who had broken an expensive antique and was trying to prove his innocence by crying. He had lost weight and was looking weaker.

'What happened to dad? He has become frail,' Jyotika asked when she arrived home.
'Stress baby! He will be alright don't worry, Mohan uncle has parted, he is sad and devastated, feeling as if he is cheated. He needs emotional support, spend some time with him.'

32

*S*unny and Koyal went to Stuttgart for honeymoon.

Almost at the time when Rainbow team was on a foreign tour.

Stuttgart, a place which was full of tranquility and natural beauty.

Simple people with smile and love.

Sunny had read in the newspaper about Rainbow musical show in Frankfurt, Stuttgart.

What a coincidence!

Sunny's decision to marry Koyal was a compromise he knew, circumstances over-power everything. Later, he realized that.

The decision was made in haste.

He could have waited for Jyotika for some more time.

Koyal was a great girl but Jyotika was the one whom he had loved since childhood, dreamt of her as a life partner.

Jyotika was famous, earned a lot of money, all by herself, supporting musical team.

They came back from honeymoon.

Koyal noticed that he always talked about his past life with Jyotika.

Koyal initially didn't react but later, she felt hurt and didn't know what to do. That was destined to happen, now what could have been done? That's life! She had given up all her career, time and investments for him and his company, had stood by him when he needed the most, married when he wanted, what else she could have done to make Sunny happy? She was a model, a stunning beauty, who fell in love with Sunny, that was her fault! She loved him, who had loved someone else.

The crack in their fragile relationship was obvious. Koyal knew, things would be better one day. It was a tough time, almost every marriage had to go through such phases nowadays . . .

She knew things would fall at the right place, one day.

Jyotika was sad ever since she had come from foreign trip. Joy was sad too. There was a media conference after they came back, followed by a cocktail party.

The musical group had become famous and many event companies were approaching them for shows in different cities in India.

Menka took a call on that, since Jyotika couldn't arrive in time. Mainly, two event companies were interested in the show, 'Music world' and 'Rhythm'.

Music world' was owned by Devesh Khanna.
Khanna talked arrogantly and promised big PR publicity.

'No Indian singer or musical band have achieved what you guys have, many Indians and Asians have tried to become famous globally . . .' He took a pause after praising them.
'You guys have more challenges ahead to maintain the position you have got for that we need publicity on a continuous basis, a strategy, PR company, events which will keep broadcasting you on news channels.' He took a pause. Menka was listening patiently.
Khanna further added, 'We are the one who have been doing the job for 35 years . . .'Khanna had powerpoint presentation of almost half an hour and showed how this can be done.

Menka wasn't very impressed. Khanna was cunning and over-smart in his approach. She heard him and told that she would revert soon.

Rhythm, was headed by a young girl named Simran Acharya. Who took over company (Rhythm) after death of her parents, in an accident. She was honest in her deals and pleaded to Menka if Rainbow joined hands with her she would try and give her best.

'I will love to be a part of the team I sing also. Please consider my proposal I have a team of experienced people who have been doing PR jobs for years. I am unable to pay salary to them after my parents' demise. Help me aunty.' She had tears in her eyes. Menka became emotional and tears rolled on her cheeks.

Menka felt as if she is seeing Bosky sitting in front of her pleading.

'Ok you have got it, my dear'. Her voice deteriorated, shattered as if she would cry, she did. She went inside the room. Everyone was quiet.

No one knew what happened.

Menka came out of the room after a while.

She had washed her face and was smiling.

'Sorry, I became emotional, you are in, very much part of our team, start working from now, guys introduce yourselves.'

Jyotika was conveyed the decision when she came to them.

Everyone supported the decision made by Menka. They also wanted Menka to take over as a leader and not Jyotika.

Jyotika was angry and didn't like the decision to go with Rhythm; as she knew that Khanna's company wanted to tie up with them. When she heard that the decision was made without her, she was very upset and expressed it too.

'Who made the decision?'

'Menka Aunty, we all supported it. You didn't show up in time, what to do?' Joy explained.

'Why no one waited for me?' Jyotika objected with authority, which she didn't know that she had lost by then.

'Simran is the right choice, she is like you guys, she needed support as she has lost her parents,' Menka replied on behalf of everyone.

Jyotika smelt, the wave was against her. She found herself alone. 'Khanna's company is old and professional, Rhythm is new' Jyotika argued.

'It's not new, it may not be as old as Khanna's company, but Simran's father had run the company for a longer time; and she is trying to revive it. She may be young, but she is honest and is offering us good deal,' Rehman tried to prove it right.

'Well, in that case, I won't be a part of this event,' Jyotika announced her decision. 'Simran or Jyotika choose one between the two'.

Jyotika was shocked that, no one budged from their places to say, 'no stay back, why are you saying that, we can explain . . .' nothing happened like that.

A pin drop silence.
She looked at Joy.
Joy was looking down on floor, not ready to look into her eyes.

She left them immediately.

It was a new beginning for Rainbow group next morning. Everyone started their practice in a new place, Menka bought the entire floor of 3,500 square feet in Bandra Kurla Complex (BKC), the most expensive commercial place in Mumbai.

Simran was the happiest girl on the planet, she found the group as her family, Menka was the decision maker for everything.

Simran was innovative; she introduced some comic items during the program. She was an aspiring singer, everyone liked her voice. She began singing songs sung by Bosky. They also recorded some new songs. Life began to rock for everyone once again.

33

*T*he beach was dark at eight at night. Iqbal, Joy's new driver was waiting for him. He bought some peanuts to pass time. He was happy joining a new job, he had heard Joy's songs, seen him singing on television many a times. He knew he was driving a star singer.

He was different, asked many bizarre questions.
'What happened to the car?'
'I think the wire connection of battery is disconnected, it might have burnt,' Robert replied after checking the bonnet.
'Where is it?' Joy wanted to know.
'Here sir.'
'Ok, and what is this?' He asked about radiator'.
'It is called radiator, sir.'
What was wrong with his boss? How come he didn't know these small things about car he was owning an expensive car like BMW and didn't know even these basics! It was his second week, he met everyone.

The most respected person who made decisions mostly was Menka madam.

He saw from a distance Joy was quiet and looking at the Chowpatty beach.

It wasn't easy to forget Jyotika. Joy was sad for her. She had hurt him many times during the show. She didn't make any call after she left. They thought she would realize her mistake and come back, but she didn't. Joy knew that, she was a tough girl, no matter what, but she was the one who united everyone for Rainbow.

He came home late night.
Menka was in the balcony.
'Come Joy,' Menka looked at him.
'What should we do with that amount?'
'Which amount?'
'Jyotika's share of amount.'

Joy didn't say anything. He knew, Menka had decided to part with Jyotika, she wouldn't have the same place even if she came back in the team. Menka was unhappy with Jyotika.

Simran's PR was good.
She organized media interview, where journalists also asked personal questions.

'Have you ever loved anyone? These songs you have sung are romantic and passionate,' asked one of the reporters, when Joy was being interviewed. The reporter wanted some story out of it, it was a live show.
'These songs are not mine. These are written by Ray you all know that. We just sing them, but yes I love someone definitely.'
'Who is she?' Joy didn't know what to say.
Jyotika might be watching the interview what to say now? Should he? Shouldn't he reveal the true feelings in front of whole world? Joy decided to be honest.
'Her name is Jyotika. She showed me this world. I am not sure, whether she loves me or not. I love her.' Joy became emotional; he had tears in his eyes.
This was what the reporter wanted, he got it.
He wanted some more form the scoop.
'Do you have any message to give her?'
'I love her, and always will . . . no matter what comes up.' The print media also took the story, it was open in public.
The Rainbow team did not want to react on it.

'Any publicity is good publicity. It's ok.' Menka announced with a smile being naughty. The team knew that, one person who is always happy and wanted to live life to the fullest, was none other than Menka.

The media called many times to publish her side of the story, she refused the offer and chose to remain silent.

She was quietly watching the news.
Joy called her. She didn't pick the call.
Joy sent a sms to her.
'It was all an honest confession, straight from the heart.'
Joy got a reply immediately.
'Honest n' straight from the heart to get publicity, right Joy?' Joy read the sms, he didn't know what to say, she was offended.
'Sorry if you think like that, I still love you, I didn't intend to hurt you.'
'You should have understood, these emotions are too personal and shouldn't have been aired through media. All the best for your new friend Simran; or your new girlfriend I should rather say! Old friends are left and dumped when one gets new ones.' Jyotika was not ready to listen to him.
What does he thinks of himself? Who are they? A bunch of jokers without her!
'Whatever you say Jyotika, I respect you, love you. Please come back.' Jyotika chose not to reply after that.

Joy remembered the times he spent with Jyotika.
He acknowledged many things as the earth is covered with water by three parts, and one part with soil, the roads are made by crushed stones. Also they pour a mixture on it to make a solid road, unbreakable, and tires can run on the road. Just by switching on a button, the darkness in the room erases?
Where does it disappear?

Internet, camera, everything magical, but she explained everything to him.

Jyotika found her dad very lonely and alone. She tried to spend time with him. Charu Jyotika and Pratap became one family for the first time.

'I want an empty room.' Jyotika asked her mother.

'It's your home, choose the one you want.' Charu was happy to see her interest.

She chose the first floor hall, called the sound engineer and asked him to convert the hall into a mini theatre.

She bought thousand DVDs most of which were of comic movies.

She used to bring gather everyone there and three of them watched movies together. She used to sit with her dad holding his hand, resting his head on her shoulder, Pratap used to rub his forehead with affection.

Charu felt the house turning into a home.

Her parents left all the decisions on her; She, most of the time was inside her room, sleeping or watching films, asking her dad, mom to barge in and to give her company. The media story didn't change her at all.

News channels, entertainments channels, newspapers were full of speculations about Joy and Jyotika's love story.

'What has happened now, why has Jyotika changed?' Simran asked Menka. While Menka was walking on peaceful road of Bandra Kurla Complex with her the other day.

'Change is rule of the nature; the world is changing every moment.' Menka said with great grave and sincerity.

Simran was friendly with everyone, she was very close to Menka.

She was amazed with the reply. She knew Menka aunty by now, her statements are thoughtful. She knew life, she had seen though times. An absolute resilient iron lady having lovely smiling face.

Joy joined them. He looked at Simran she smiled and he responded with smile.

Joy found her sweet and friendly, when she spoke slowly, chewing words with clear diction.

'You speak well.' Joy spoke to her. Menka was listening with smile. She knew, Jyotika's place in Joy's heart will be filled by Simran.

'I didn't say a word wasn't I quiet aunty?'

'Yes you were, I completely agree with you.' Menka supported having enjoyed the very moment.

'I am not talking about this very moment, I say generally you speak well whenever you speak'.

'O really?'

Joy didn't have an answer.

They walked that night for a longer time under open sky. There was coffee shop opened till late night. They had coffee and came back home.

Joy felt good in Simran's company. Menka wanted them to come close. Jyotika had gone far without any response.

Simran had the habit of giving surprises.

'What's in my left hand?' She had asked, next day when she came.

'I don't know.'

'I know, you don't know, its a surprise for you'.

Joy kept on guessing. He couldn't, finally she opened her fist.

'Its empty!' Joy saw nothing in it.

'Air. It has air.'

Everyone around laughed.

Simran was the one who was making the team vibrant.

She had a fabulous sense of humour.

She was with him because Joy wanted to know about things.

'No one wants these answers who have vision. Why people are hardly interested to know about things?' Joy was always surprised to think that. Joy never thought that a time will come, when she would reply on sms so harshly. He couldn't do anything about that, he knew that, these things were part of life.

34

*T*ime flew fast.

Simran became darling of the team and Jyotika stayed out.
Vandy and Rehman got married. Manoj Jain met a girl called
Anamika, an Indo - African Singer, who joined the team too. Jyotika
was called by Menka one day. Jyotika decided to meet her, she thought,
the life might take a turn and things might work again. She was ready to
forget and forgive everything happened.

Jyotika went to the new office for the first time. Everything had
changed. Menka's cabin was huge, attached to the rehearsal hall. It looked
like a clean, French marble finished, beautiful, well-furnished home,
rather than an office. Jyotika's eyes searched for joy. He wasn't there.

'How are you?' Menka welcomed her with a soothing pleasant smile.
She hugged Jyotika. Both sat on a white stone turned into a sofa with
cushions on it.

'How are you?' Menka asked.

Jyotika smiled in reply.

'Coffee?' Menka asked again. Jyotika smiled again. She asked the
serving boy to bring coffee.

'You look very pretty aunty!' Jyotika praised. Menka blushed.

They praised each other, talked about media promotion, music, Rainbow and the weather of Mumbai, changing scenario of music world, new hits.

They had general conversation which halted with a silence. Time to talk about the issue, she was called for. 'Jyotika,' Menka broke the ice.

'You didn't come to collect your money, I therefore, made a cheque without asking you.' Menka got up to bring the cheque kept on the glass table. Jyotika was expecting anything but not this.

She didn't say a word.

Everything was changed. She met a professional, not Menka aunty.

Jyotika's car was running out of Bandra-Kurla-Complex, she was lost in thoughts, didn't realize that, driver was asking where to drive down.

She actually didn't know where to go from there.

The driver took her home anyway.

'This envelope was laying on the back seat of the car,' the driver gave the envelope to Pratap. He opened it. It was a cheque of 20 million, with Jyotika's name printed on it.

He showed it to Charu and discussed about it on dinner table.

'Is this cheque yours?' Pratap asked.

'Which cheque?'

'The driver had given me an envelope today.'

'Oh that, how much is that?'

'You don't know?'

Jyotika nodded her head in negative.

'I am fixing that amount in your name.'

'You can use it if you want.' Jyotika was least interested in money. She had seen enough, she knew it could buy her things she wanted to.

The rainbow team continued their shows from one city to another, they started with Jaipur and later performed at Agra, Delhi, Chandigarh, Bhopal and Pune.

Jyotika had nothing to do with that. She watched the promotional news of Rainbow, which was going on without her. Charu tried to talk to her, but her reply was always short, unwilling to say anything.

That Sunday she decided to sleep after having lunch. She had rice and curry, her favorite meal. She went to sleep in her room.

She rested for almost two hours.

She got up in the evening, it was five. She didn't want to get up from the bed, feeling lazy. She let herself on the bed. She decided to read some of Ray's poetry. She opened his old diary. She saw her photos with Ray, both of them were smiling. She smiled seeing that. Her life became impossible after his death. She began to read one of the poems . . ..

Smile Please!
Stones melt,
Earth giggles,
Soil welcomes,
Hills shake,
Nature gets wet
Rain drops sing.
I am asking you not to
walk an extra mile,
but to smile!
So, smile please.

She read the lines again and again.
'No one can take his place, my Ray's place! Joy is his shadow, not him, he can't be him.'
She actually got confused with shadow and reality.
'Joy is a shadow, yes he is!' She repeated this again and again, so that she was sure about her decision, that she had made a right decision of leaving him and leaving the entire group.' Charu entered her room.
'Coffee, beta?'
'Yes please, I really need it.'
Charu left her alone. She knew that it would be fine, if she was alone and happy. Her face was glowing, means she had a sound sleep. She

needed good care and love from her; it was the time when Jyotika needed her mom.

Ray was addicted to tea, he started having coffee when she insisted. Ray was a great man. He went away leaving Rainbow behind. He had written songs, and after him, all his songs were being sung all over the world.

Charu put the coffee mug in front of her and cuddled her head with love. She smiled. There was something cropped up, which she should be told.

'Someone has come, waiting for you, saying that he is friend and knows you very well.' Charu informed her.

'Who? Didn't he tell his name?'

'He says your phone is switched off, he has been trying it since two hours. Is your phone switched off?' Jyotika switched her phone on and started getting phone call alerts. He was none other than Mark.

'Mark!' She got up, ran out to see him. Charu was definitely surprised. A new man in her daughter's life, from London!

'Hi! You?' She hugged him.

'Ya, It's me, thought I should see you.'

'Ok, why didn't you call me? I could have come to the airport to pick you up.'

'I wanted to surprise you and I wouldn't have, if I would have known this kind of enthusiastic hug I would get.' He said with a naughty smile.

Jyotika took him inside the house. She was holding his hand, very happy and excited. Mark was rather feeling little embarrassed. He had no idea, who would meet him; and how he or she would treat him, seeing their daughter so mad, happy and excited.

'He is Mark mom . . . and . . .'

'She is your elder sister!' Mark was flirting.

'How did you know, that?' Jyotika smiled.

'She is so beautiful, anyone can guess!' Charu blushed.

'She is my mother and not sister, you failed.'

'Have I? Oh my God! You look so fit! You are her sister she must be joking!'

She was not expecting that, this evening will bring so much happiness for the family. Jyotika was sad all these days, and the entire family was sad because of that.

Jyotika didn't stop there, she entered inside her room with Mark, showing her the house. She saw the diary lying on the bed. She took the diary and kept it on the table. A big size Ray's portrait was enhancing the room's beauty.

'I am here for one day. I am hosting a show with Bollywood stars. I will have to leave tomorrow.' Mark said. He knew that he should say something to her to begin the conversation. Both were looking at each other and not talking at all.

'You have come here according to your wish, but Mr. Mark Robin you will leave Mumbai according to my wish, is that clear?'

'But . . .'

'It's final, no ifs, no buts.'

'Yes mam!'

'Tell me one thing where is everyone? I want to invite everybody for my show,' Mark changed the topic.

'Whom are you looking for? Whom do you mean by everyone?'

'Your Musical team, Rainbow.'

'It's no more my team; the team has changed,.That's what life is, change is mandatory. I left the team and I am happy being myself, Jyotika Sanyal, Just me!'

'Hmm . . .' He tried to understand.

They kept on talking. They left for the show, anchored by Mark with many other film stars. Late at night, they decided to go for a drive. Jyotika was driving; the road was almost empty.

'If I say you are different . . .' Mark began to talk.

'I am different . . . means? How different and which way?'

'Different from what you were, during your tour. Correct me if I am wrong!'

'I do not know what to say. Candidly speaking, I realized later that, I made a wrong choice. I thought he is . . . Leave it! Why we are discussing someone else, past is past, said and done; finished! I am looking ahead and trust me I want to be happy Mark. I am happy today, I am very happy to see you.'

'I understand everything, allow me to say something, I knew they were using you.'

'Forget them Mark. It's Ok. They have moved ahead and so am I.'

They came back at around 2 O'clock in the morning.

Pratap Sanyal was awake and was waiting to see the new guest. Charu had briefed him about Mark. Pratap became very happy to see him, as he could now say with pride that, his son-in-law was someone from London, from a reputed family. An Indian, settled in UK.

He was the happiest man that day. Pratap didn't want to miss the opportunity to announce their marriage, unless Jyotika said that they had to wait. Pratap didn't want to wait, but he could do nothing about it.

Mohan Kumar meanwhile decided to join hands with his son Sunny. His company merged into Sunny's company. Koyal didn't want that but she thought she shouldn't say anything. Soon the differences cropped up.

Their working methods didn't match. Koyal gave up. She was unhappy. Sunny was drunk most of the times, day and night. He was least interested in anything; business was left to God's mercy.

One day early in the morning Koyal tried to make him understand. She brought tea in the bedroom, Sunny was reading newspaper.

'You look fresh and great this morning,' Koyal said and kissed him, Sunny kissed her back without a word.

Sunny had become mechanical. Most of the time lost in thoughts; he only responded when she said something or else asked her when she was needed for things like-

"Have you seen this? I can't find these things."
"Where is my file?"
"I am going for this meeting".
"Can you sort this out?"
"I don't understand why dad is like that, please talk to him" etc . . .

Sunny was never like that. He was ardent, energetic, enthusiastic, punctual, careful, alert, responsible, caring, sharing, a type professional.

But he had become became lazy, she didn't know what to say, what to do? How could she make him understand?

Sunny used to be with her, make love, but there was something missing, may be the romance? More than romance, emotions . . .

She wanted to try to talk about that today, early in the morning.

'Should I say something Sunny?'

'Ya, go ahead, I am listening,' he said while reading the newspaper.

'Could you please put the newspaper aside?'

'Ya, tell me now,' Sunny threw the newspaper.

'What's wrong Sunny?'

'Nothing, what's wrong? I do not know? Has anything gone wrong?'

'Our relationship is losing emotions; emotion of true love, romance. We are losing essence of it, don't you think that?'

'I never realized anything of that sort, honestly speaking Koyal.'

'That's what the thing is. You never realize anything, why? Why Sunny?'

'Tell me, what am I supposed to do?'

'Why don't you understand? Why do I need to tell you, what you are supposed to do? It's you, who will call the shots not me.' Sunny didn't say anything. He was quiet. Koyal shut him up. He knew it. He knew what the problem was. Sooner or later this was going to happen, he knew that. It was happening then, was bound to happen.

'See, we meet only on bed, otherwise there is no talk, love, emotion, romance, smile, laughter, sharing, caring, jokes, nothing happens like that.'

'Do you want an honest answer?' Sunny wanted to speak then.

'I want an honest relationship Sunny.'

'You need honest confession for an honest relationship, do you agree?' She nodded in 'yes'.

'I do not find purpose in life. My dream has come to an end. I don't know what should I do, what for? For whom? I have always dreamt a life with someone, you also know that. I can't find her around, and do not know the reason why can't she be here for me? I have failed. I don't know where I will go from here . . .' She listened patiently.

'Well now after listening to you, you might not be willing to hear this news, but I am pregnant.' Time paused for a moment, for both of them.

Sunny didn't know how to react.

35

Mark was in touch through internet and phone messaging. They had general conversations, Mark was under the impression that she would marry Joy. He knew everything.

Jyotika knew if Mark could stay back for a week, he would stay back in her life forever.

Mark was having fun with Jyotika. He was very happy and didn't want to go, leaving her alone.

The darkness had gripped with moon light. They had dinner and were ready for a walk. Both of them began to walk on Worli sea face.

'I will leave tomorrow' Mark initiated the talk.

Jyotika didn't say much, rather she just said,'Oh!'

'I have asked my travel agent to book the ticket,'

Mark further conveyed the plan.

'Hmm . . .' Jyotika heard it right.

What's the big deal? Anyways the travel agent will have to book the ticket without which he can't go! The ticket has to be booked, rubbish!

These boys waste girls' time and make them think a lot. What to say now? How to say? What's the difficulty you idiot! Say clearly. Why is he dragging it? What is the point in talking irrelevant things, Jyotika's mind started pondering over thoughts.

'The area in which you live is really great. The sea looks fantastic from here.'

'Oh my god!' She was pissed off,

Come to the point you dolt! Don't you know what to say?

'I think we should go; I am feeling sleepy,' Jyotika lost her patience.

'Stay for some more time; see the full moon.' She knew it, he was waiting for the right time. Why is he dragging things? Talking about moon and the sea. He can be romantic after having proposed her, she couldn't wait to hear the golden words from his mouth.

'You know Jyotika, I never ever thought we will walk late on the Worli sea face in Mumbai. I think God had planned something for us.'

Yes, he is on his way to say, pronounce his discourse now, he is making ground for that. So what have God planned for us? Tell me go ahead you dumb. What's his problem? What is the fear all about? Say whatever you want to say, love you, hate you, wan'na marry you, wan'na stay in live-in relationship, come with me to London again, say something . . ., Jyotika was excited like a college girl.

'See, I am really feeling sleepy!' Jyotika took a final call. Okay!.

Idiot! Doesn't understand tomorrow he is going, so when will he get a chance to propose me? Never! May be he will call me from London and say it on phone.'

'Wait a minute,' He stopped her.

She was ready and was waiting to be stopped by him.

'Jyotika, would you like to come to London with me?'

'I had been to London once, remember? We met in London during our shows and I have seen London.'

'No, I mean forever? Together, to spend the rest of our lives . . .'

'Hmm! Not a bad idea!'

'Are you planning to start some new business?'

'No - no . . . I . . . I'

'Why are you fumbling?'

'I am not . . .' Mark was sweating. An anchor who never feared any time, faced thousands of eyes while addressing the audience, was nervous. She could see that.

'Are you coming?'

'Where?' She pretended.

'London?'

'For what? I said I have been to London before many times, once with you also. I have been in fact visiting London ever since I was two!'

'I mean . . .'

'You are not clear Mark; say what do you wanna say? I am confused. I know you love me but why London?' She pretended again.

Mark smiled. He knew she was pulling his leg, but why she was doing that? Was she making fun of him?
'I wanna marry you, I love you' Mark then finally proposed her.
'That's what you wanted to say?'
'You can kiss me.'
'Sorry? What? Here?'
'Here, yes! People come here to kiss each other. This place is known as lovers' point.'

The wedding of Jyotika and Mark was announced as a very big event, while the Rainbow musical team was traveling, having shows in different cities.

Sunny was about to become a father.

Jyotika was getting married to Mark.
The marriage was in London and a huge reception was thrown at Mumbai. Pratap Sanyal flaunted his money and power to the world to show, how rich marriages happen.

36

The Rainbow team came back from the 2nd tour. Joy was sad, very sad, upset with Jyotika as she didn't even tell him that, she was getting married. Menka was very busy in setting up a new recording studio; whatever they had earned had been invested in building a studio in Bandra-Kurla-Complex. Simran had become an integral part of their team. The studio was inaugurated by famous singers and renowned people from the film industry.

They announced that, after a successful venture of Rainbow, they would be launching a new video album called Rainbow 2, and the entire group will be seen in the video as singing and performing.

It was Simran's idea which was liked by everyone.
Menka was happy that Simran was taking interest in it. Both of them sang very well and when they sang duets, audience went crazy.

Menka asked Joy to talk to a Jaipur - based company who wanted to appear as a main sponsor. Joy and Simran left for the venture.

The flight arrived at Jaipur in the afternoon.
They reached to the hotel. It was a palace, which was converted into a hotel.

'There has been room booked?' Joy asked. The receptionist checked the computer, looking at him.

'Yes, sir Rainbow . . . Joy?'

'Ya' Joy smiled.

'Sir how many rooms do you want? It's not mentioned here'.

Joy who was facing the receptionist, thought for a moment about what to answer.

He looked at Simran.

'One deluxe room, ok!' Simran replied from the back. She came closer to Joy and smiled.

'May I have your autograph please?' Joy heard a voice when he was about to leave for his room. A beautiful girl was smiling.

'Sure why not?' He took out his pen.

'What's your name?'

'Pallavi.' He signed with her name beside, wishing her luck. Simran looked at the girl, Simran came closer to Joy to show that, he is with her.

Receptionist was still observing them.

They entered the huge room. More than double spaced.

It looked like a real palace, facing a huge river.

Simran looked outside the window opening it ajar.

'Awesome! Isn't it a great view?' Joy moved few steps to see.

'Ya, it is.'

She turned and found that Joy was standing right behind her, she was about to push him, he came very close to see what she was looking outside the window. Joy didn't budge. For a fraction of second their faces faced each other, eyes exchanged encounters.

Joy takes one step back. She moved to left. Her sleeveless hand rubbed Joy's hand. She felt the vibration inside. She sat on the huge chair looked antique, more than a chair, everything in the room was large in size.

Jaipur was hot in day time.

The evening was soothing, Pleasant, peaceful, palaces, buildings had one color - pink, cycle rickshaw, broad roads, people wearing turbans on head. Simple honest people offering services to visitors.

They hired a cab and went to see few locations, mostly palaces and their history, forts, hills and bravery stories blended with love stories.

They wanted to spend memorable time together.
Simran clicked their photographs having her hands stretched.
'Excuse me!' Joy called a couple.
'Would you please click some of our photographs?'
The man was busy clicking their pictures while his wife was looking at Joy.
'May I have a picture with you?' His wife requested.
'Off course!'
The entire crowed then surrounded Joy for a photo session. Simran was pushed aside. She looked at Joy without any expression, but smile. She was happy to have a person like Joy beside her, who was a great singer and everyone loved him.

They came back around 8 pm and entered the room. Simran went inside the bathroom and came out with freshness. Joy saw her completely. She was fair, very fair, long hair, big eyes, big bosoms, slim wrist, a sexy appearance, a beautiful dame. She had worn short skirt and sleeveless top.

'Don't you wanna get fresh, or you just wanna stare at me like that, as if you have never seen girl before?' Simran asked him when he was staring at her.
'A half naked girl!' Joy commented.
'How sick, bad joke again. Who is half naked you backward mind!'
'I didn't say full, only said half.' He smiled.
'Say, don't stop, I wanna see your perverted mind.'
Joy didn't say, laughed loudly and went inside the bathroom.

Joy and Simran had great chemistry as singers.
They sang in a high pitch and audience held their breath while they sang.

Nothing would have changed, if Simran entered in his life. He thought.
Life is like that, one person enters another exits, emotions kill people, few respect emotions, many misuse them. He was growing with life's realities, hard facts, naked truths.

Bosky who contracted to kill him was in love with him as she claimed, was that love?!

He loved Jyotika, she loved Mark.

He came out in white bathrobe. Simran looked at him, he was sure she would smile, she did smile . . .

He wore white plain T shirt and loose pyajama. He looked decent in white dress he knew that.

'Let's go for dinner, I am feeling hungry what about you?' Joy offered, applied deodorant in his armpit and neck.

The dinner hall was big, waiters serving having turbans and Pajamas with long Kurtas. Jaipur is known for kings. The concept the hotel was based on the tradition and culture.

They ordered looking at the menu.

They enjoyed the music and seeing each other.

One of the waiters came running who was watching them for a long time.

'Hello sir I am your huge fan. How did you like the meal?' Joy smiled.

'Thanks! It is good.'
'You have a God gifted voice sir.'
'Thank you, brother.'
They came to the room after a walk in hotel campus besides the swimming pool.

'Coffee?' Joy asked.
'Of course! Black!'

He dialed and ordered for a cup of coffee.

'So, what's your story?' Simran asked without delay.
'You know my story. Simple, ends in one sentence, an orphan who was blind, now a half blind got famous for his singing skills, trying to understand love, emotion, passion and life.' Joy explained.

'I know this story, everyone was talking about your previous life, Menka aunty told me about it. What's your love story?'

'There was none, I loved Jyotika, thought she also loved me, she choses to marry Mark and flew to London'.

'Humm! Smart way to brief, you should be a writer,' Simran smiled.

'God is the writer, I am just briefing it.'

The waiter came with coffee. They waited for him to leave, both of them sipped the coffee. Both of them were silent.

'What's your story?' Joy showed interest to know.

'Are you really interested to know, or just passing time?' Simran asked.

'Both, why are you worried anyway, you do not want to share, it's fine then. Let's have sex and sleep.' Joy teased her.

'You wanna have sex with me really, or just teasing me?'

'What do you think, a wild guess?'

'I don't wanna guess, you tell me I have asked the question, you got to answer me.' Simran was ardent.

'If I say I wanna have sex with you? How would you react?'

'Why should I react?'

Joy failed to understand Simran.

'Ok, I will toss, heads sex tails no sex, only conversation, what say?' Joy bounced a proposal.

'It's your call boss! Your coin, you wish to toss, what can I say? I am supposed to say nothing, I will only respond when something comes concrete, beyond hypothetical assumption.' Simran made her point clear.

'Ok! Lets see!'

Joy tossed, he saw it. Simran was quiet, smiling. Joy looked at the coin, looked at her, smiled. Finally, sais:

'Its a tail'.

She smiled, she didn't bother to see the coin.

'The coin says, let's talk, tell me your love story.'

Simran took a deep breath.

'His name is Pawan Malhotra. We were together in college. We had planned each and everything, the flat, the kitchen set up, our marriage date, everything,' She sipped the coffee.

'I trusted him completely. Everything changed after the death of my parents, he came to know that my dad's company had bank liabilities. He stopped meeting me. He met someone called Chaitali. Everything happened fast when I visited his house one day, Chaitali was in his bedroom. My photograph had been removed from his bedroom table. He said he is in love with Chaitali. Story ended there.'

Simran was serious and sad while telling the story. She finished the coffee and continued the story.

'I was depressed and down I decided to revive my dad's company. It looked almost impossible.'

She had tears in her eyes. She went to the window looked out side the river.

Joy got up, touched her cheeks and smiled, caught her hand, made her seat on the same chair.

'Then, what happened after that?'

'I met Menka aunty and Joy.'

'Who is Joy?'

'He is an arrogant singer. Thinks, he is the only talented person in this world,' she said lightly to release the heavy stress of the past.

'Why do you think so? I know he is not, Joy is humble, polite, why don't you check and make your facts right'

'I will one day, when I will grow old.'

'Really, do you have that much patience?'

'I think I have.'

'Hmm!' Joy looked at her.

'Life is like that what to do?' Joy said again.

'Ya, I Know, what to do?' She tried to smile.

'Where is he now? Pawan?'

'He had called up last week, I was surprised to see his number, I called him back, he said sorry, was regretting his decision. Later, I came to know that Chaitali had left him too.'

Silence for some moment.

'You guys have given a new life to me. I never thought I will sing professionally, that became possible because of Menka aunty who has great eyes to see the talent.' She became emotional.

'. . .And I know It was a heads, not a tails.' She said having tears in her eyes.

Joy smiled, she had seen the coin, He was having fun, passing time and getting her close as friend, but it seemed she had come closer.

They saw each other standing at the window. The river water was shining.

Next morning, Joy opened his eyes, he was sleeping on one part of the bed, Simran was in the bathroom, he thought.
The tea tray was kept there, he made a cup of tea for himself.
Got up, walked down to the window again. The river water was clean and pure.

Joy and Simran arrived in time at the office, Anurag Agarwal was very decisive and quick in making decisions.

'I love music, I am your big fan. I am doing this for passion rather than business. You guys have my support whenever wherever you want me'. He offered them whatever best he could.

Menka was very happy to see that they have made a great deal, Menka personally called Anurag and thanked him.

The preparation began for all India event, which was to initiate from East, Odisha, Kolkota, Bhubaneswar, Gauhati and many other places.
Menka became the busiest person on earth. Office and rehearsal halls, managing finance.

It was mandatory to happen . . .She fell ill.
Dr. Khanna suggested her to take rest, it was happening because of exertion.

37

*I*n the evening, Menka was resting in her bedroom. She had medicines and slept for almost five hours. She didn't want to get up or go anywhere.

After Ray, Simran and Joy had become her breath and soul. Bosky's jealousy led her to a devastating end. Jyotika left them; the passion of music and life didn't stop.

Today, they were known! Rainbow was famous. Ray couldn't die . . .
She looked at Ray's photo, he was smiling.
A lonely woman, came so far from nowhere, Menka thought.

Life teaches everyone a lesson, some learn and many don't.
The journey has no end but it ends one day . . .

She loved music, her family, her husband, son everyone. She found meaning of life in music. Ray was a great poet, a genius, who was killed; and the world knew his story. Even she is known today.

Being famous meant nothing to her, but for life itself being famous means a lot, people want to be rich and famous.

She picked up some of the poems from the collection. She read a few lines of the poem:

Let your wings move

Let's fly
Do not feel shy,
let's fly.
Spread your wing,
Punch your ankle,
Feel high.
Try . . .
Try to fly high.

Amazing inspiring thoughts.
She thought, she should publish a book.
'Yes! It will be a real tribute to Ray and his work. Let me fly high' is a good title.'
God had his own planning; she was so busy that she had forgotten Ray completely. The idea was liked by the team.

Meanwhile, Anurag Agarwal visited Mumbai and met everyone. He invited the team to perform at Pune, where he was opening a new branch office.

Pune's show was classic. They sung the new songs.
Menka for the first time read Ray's poems on stage-

I didn't know how to fly,
Wings were weak.
I had to go beyond peak.
I fell down.
Drowned . . .in the deep sea,
I repented the endeavor.
Wings pained.
Down I, and no gain.
A fresh breeze
Touched me again.
I crawled back,

I tightened my wings.
Live or fly,
Decided to
Die, if I couldn't fly.
I flew,
in sky above the hills,
I spread my wings.
Made mountains small.
High up was the sky.
I knew, many heights still untouched.
I wanna touch.
I wanna touch.

The applaud resounded in the hall and was not stopping.

'My son never died, you all have proved that, your love for Ray's poems has proved that.' Menka broke down over the people's response. She had tears in her eyes. An unexpected happy moment.

'This poetry would take the shape of a book'. Anurag Agarwal immediately announced that, 'my company will publish the book **'Let me fly high'.'** Anurag went on the dais took the mike and said.

Anurag had the book publishing company also, which had distribution network throughout the world. Menka was never so much excited in her entire life like that day. Menka's excitement was like a 18 yr old girl.

She was jumping, kissing and hugging everyone; she behaved as if she was a young girl.

Simran, Joy and Menka arrived at Jaipur as Anurag Agarwal's guests. They saw the design of the book. Anurag was a scholar himself. He wrote an emotional write up that, his journey of success became very small when he read Ray's poetry which spoke and lit up life's philosophy with candid approach.

Menka wrote about Ray on the second page with a photograph of Menka and Ray, in which Ray had hugged her with smile and love. Joy didn't miss to mention that, this life was given to him as a re-birth by Ray.

There were quotations from everyone about the book and Ray. They came back to Mumbai. The day for the launch of the book was decided.

Soon, the day came. It was a very big event. Anurag was very influential, he invited politicians, film stars, social personalities, famous writers and intellectuals for the occasion. The huge venue was full of media people.

It was very a emotional moment for Menka, she had tears in her eyes. She broke down and cried while making her speech.

'. . . I don't know what to say, from where to begin, this has no end . . . Our Rainbow was once called, a dark Rainbow! Anyone who wants to live, never dies. Ray never died. He lives with us every moment, he lives in Joy, He lives in his music. I wish you all to live life sensible paired with greatness.

I want to live in painting and Joy wants to live in his singing.

'I thank everyone, specially Mr. Anurag Agarwal, a generous man, who has great respect for art and culture. He loves music. God bless him who supports people like us, who came from nowhere!'
She took a pause, 'I feel contended after publishing Ray's book, 'Let me fly high,' I can fly to God now, I am ready . . .Trust me I am ready, with all my wishes fulfilled.

I love you all. At this moment I have also forgiven people who killed my son. I know who are they, God bless them too . . .'

Anurag Agarwal sitting at the front row had tears in his witnessing an emotional speech of an emotional mother, straight from her heart.

The sun rose in the east this morning too.
Simran made tea and entered Menka's room. She screamed. The cup fell down on the floor and broke in to pieces. Joy was the first to reach to the room. Menka was sleeping calmly, without any breath running. Joy froze at his place and couldn't believe that, she was no more with them.

Joy did her last rites as her son, when she was being cremated. A very important chapter of his life ended. But the show should have continued . . . They left as per schedule of their travel all over India, starting from the eastern states.

Joy was happy for Menka, she lived her life and left it with pride with all her wishes fulfilled.

'Let me fly high' hit as the best seller all over the world. It had a great sale with a great review. It had won many awards and Ray was rated as great poet in many conferences.

Anurag Agarwal's book publishing company had a great business.

38

*S*unny had heard about Menka's demise through the media news. He was frustrated with all kinds of Rainbow news.

He was the least concerned. He was drinking when the news flashed on the television.

He watched all kinds of news, this was one of them. His concern was actually nothing, nothing at all. Film celebrities, artistes, writers, painters, social workers, politicians almost everyone paid homage to Menka's death.

Koyal was pregnant, Sunny was drunk.

Mohan Kumar was unable to understand why the hell the company was making losses. Old employees of the company began to leave one by one; the new ones were not so loyal. Koyal knew this would happen; she knew Sunny's dad's method was old and couldn't sustain in this new kind of system, which was created by her and sunny.

Sunny was least interested in any business. He used to get up and slept having booze; round the clock he was drunk. He was waiting for the new guest to come, and that happened one day. He forgot everything, seeing his beautiful baby.

He promised Koyal, he wouldn't touch alcohol. His life changed completely after seeing his daughter. They decided to keep her name Pani, a new name. Pani was very cute, she always used to smile.

They were happy again. Sunny drank occasionally.

He was always with Pani, playing with her, seeing her growing, desperate to see her first step.

Sunny was at home that evening when his dad came home, sad and worried.

'We have to sell some of our properties.'

'Sell it. Tell me when and where you want my signature,' Sunny knew this would happen soon. He would earn it again, he thought. He was now not worried about anything. Koyal interrupted, 'Think of Pani, Parinita will grow one day, what kind of life we will give her, if we sell everything like that? What's wrong with the company? Why don't you take interest? Why don't you go to office and see what's wrong there?'

'This company can't be saved now. It has debts and is making losses, no one can save it,' Sunny was firm. The other day their CA Prakash Kapil warned them about the losses.

'Ok, I will save this company. I will see what's wrong. I can again make this company grow, I can do that, I will do it for my daughter Parinita'. Sunny had got purpose for his life.

Sunny called everyone in the conference room. He addressed with full energy; he tried to motivate employees, 'Nothing is impossible if we work hard.' He quoted many great leaders of the world. For a moment it seemed that he will bring back everything on track.

But, when he met the CA and the accounts department separately, his enthusiasm was no more the same. The company had sunk in the loan; banks were warning that if their money wasn't returned soon the company will face dire consequences. The private investors were unhappy with the growth of the company.

Sunny then, tried to involve some of their very close business friends. He called everyone at home and requested to help. They promised and went. No one was really ready to join hands with them. They knew that the company was running in huge debts; the ship was sinking, why someone would board on a sinking ship?

It seemed difficult; Sunny was worried. Rats run first when the ship starts sinking; both of them, Koyal and Sunny knew that.

Vinayak was the new player who entered in the difficult times. He said, 'Ramesh Mittal will buy the company; he buys old companies only and that is the only way out at that moment.'

The family of Mohan Kumar, Sunny and Koyal discussed the proposal and decided to sell it off to live a stress free life. They sold everything. Mohan Kumar suffered from a stroke; he was admitted in a hospital. He later, survived with paralysis. He was forced to live a life dependant on others. The only thing they could save was their flat and some bank balance. Sunny had to sell even, his Panchgani's bungalow, which he had built with lot of passion and had seen dreams to stay there with Jyotika.

39

*J*yotika heard Menka's news and felt sorry about the whole thing.

She called Joy and conveyed her condolences. She also said that, she should have come to see her. She wished everyone all the very best. Joy was very composed while talking to her.

'It's ok, but Menka aunty missed you a lot. It would have been great if you would have been present at the time of book release,' Joy tried to explain.

'Oh, Ray's book?'

'Let me fly high!'

It's available all over the world, Anurag Publications has published the book.' Joy informed her.

She was thrilled. 'Ray's Book! Yes! She knew, 'let me fly high'.'

She became very happy and excited to read the book.

'No one called me Joy,' Jyotika complained.

'We heard that you are married and went abroad. We didn't have access to your new number.'

'You could have tried my mom's number Joy,' Jyotika was the same, dictating everyone.

'I had taken the numbers calling Charu aunty Jyotika. Sorry! And forget not whatever has happened, let's stay in touch as friend.' Joy cooled her down.

'Ya sure, thanks Joy, how you have been? How are you?'

'Surviving. How are you?'

'Alive in a foreign country.'

'You happy?'

'I am . . .'she sounded low while repling Joy.

She missed the team now . . .five months had passed just like that! Now what? London is not her city; and also Mark didn't do anything.

He was an anchor.

'Do not get confused with shadow . . . Mark is shadow of the Rainbow team . . .' she recalled Menka's words during the world tour. She was right.

She knew why he married to her; because she is the only daughter of a millionaire, a rich girl! Mark's family had a big house. His dad was a very busy person, always traveling, mom had separated, so there was no one to manage such a big house.

What is to be done now? She didn't want to live in a city and country which was not her's. She was an Indian; she missed all that fragrance of Mumbai.

Mumbai is a great place, she missed staying there, she missed family and friends. She was emotionally attached to Mumbai. She grew there, she studied there, she met Ray in Mumbai, Menka, the music . . . passion . . . rains . . . She wanted to go back, but how? Mark was different.

She called up Mark who had gone to meet an event management company.

'Hi sweetheart, missing me?'

'Getting bored, where are you?'

'In a meeting baby, will finish it in an hour. Why don't you come down to Central Lane? We will have dinner together and go back together.'

'Ok, I am coming. I have to buy a book also. You call me once you are free.'

Jyotika was ready, she was excited to see the book. She reached 'Oxford Book Center'. She found the book in display. 'Let me fly high' could be seen prominently in the show case. She was so happy. She went to the counter and paid the amount. She came out with the book, went to the coffee shop and began to read it.

She went through her memory lane . . . The rain, Mumbai, Bandra sea link, Prithivi theatre . . . Those days . . . The music . . . Rainbow and her love Ray! Ray . . . 'A ray' of her love life . . . She submerged into book, 'Let me fly high,' she began to fly in the sky, with wings of thoughts.

Let's fly together ..

Be with me please.
When you don't be with me,
I don't be with myself.
I don't feel 'me'.
Cloud, rain and Rainbow.
I don't feel the world,
I don't feel the soil,
Sky, my existence.
Come to save my entity.
You are welcome in my life always,
You are can rest on my chest.
What are you waiting for?
Join the show baby.
Welcom to the club
Sing and smile.
. . .And we will fly,
we will fly together.
Let's fly.

She was upset and was not taking Ray's phone. Then Ray texted her from Menka's cell and sent it to her.

She read it and ran to Ray. It was raining that day, they were wet and had gone to watch a play. She came home very late that night. The next day she was not able to get up from the bed; she had high fever, cough and cold. Charu was very angry, what was she doing? Spoiling herself. She was not allowed to move out from the bed.

Ray also became sick after that. Both of them were on bed; sending messages and talking on phone . . .

'Hi!' Jyotika said.

'Hi!' Ray responded.

'Me sick.'

'Me too.'

'Mom is not letting me go out of home.'

'Same here.'

'Doctor had asked to take rest'

'Ya, true. My doctor had told me the same, so, what to do?'

'Now what?'

'Now what? You tell me, I wanna meet you.'

'You can fly, and come.'

'Get some another idea, it's raining can't fly when it rains.'

'Hmm . . .your kite can fly in the rain why can't you?'

The phone got disconnected. She tried, connection failed.

She got a poem as text message.

When things go haywire,
Without a link of wire,
Connect your heart, soul,
Call for rain;
And sing bow . . .bow . . .
Rainbow . . .

Ray called again after five minutes.

'See I am there with you, read me'

'Love you sweethaert'.

Ray was one in million. She remembered those moments; those were really best moments, best times of her life! Why was she missing them after five months of her marriage?

What was wrong with Mark?

Is this a relationship? Is it a compromised marriage? What will she do now? She needed time to think about her life. She was reading poems, preface, watching Menka's photo, Ray's photo . . .

Coffee was cold, she didn't realize that. When she put down the book and saw outside from the glass in front of her, she looked at a face. The face was familiar, yes, of course, It was Mark! Her husband. Mark was standing in front of her, angry, red faced. What happened? She was lost in Ray's poems and forgot everything for some time. She forgot Mark.

'I have been calling you since two hours, what's wrong with your phone?'

'My phone?' She was still in thoughts.

'I don't know,' she replied innocently. Mark was zapped, looking at her, what had happened to her? Where was she lost? He saw the book, 'Let me fly high,' what kind of book she was reading? He had one hundred questions in his mind.

'Sweetie are you okay? Where is your phone?'

'My phone? Ya, my phone . . .' She looked for her phone. Where it was; it was in her purse. Where was her purse? Right beside her, on the chair. She took it out from the purse; there were many missed calls. The phone was on silent mode. She remembered, she had put the phone on silent mode before she began to read the book.

'Whose book is this?' Mark looked at the book.

'Ray's book, he had written it, I mean, it has been published recently, and sold all over the world, is very popular.'

'Ya, I know, it has been nominated for the Booker prize'

'How do you know him? Who is he?'

'What to say?' Her husband was asking about Ray . . .

'What to say about Ray? He was an amazing person; he defined life in one sentence. He was a great singer, writer. He was a genius, incomparable genius! And Mark might be her husband, but Ray was always above all as far as her life was concerned.' She thought of revealing her thoughts.

'I am asking something, where have you lost baby?'

'I am lost? Ya, I really am lost.' Mark had never seen her like this.

'Let's go, we will have dinner.' They moved from there to the car. She was silent most of the time. The book had taken her in the past so effectively that, she had lost interest in present.

'Present is amazing, we should always live in present and enjoy every moment; no matter what happens in life, good or bad, doesn't matter.' She remembered Ray had always lived in present. Such a strong guy, alive after death!

Rainbow is world famous now. Ray's book is being read by the world. Ray is still amongst us!

They reached to a restaurant. Mark ordered for dinner. 'Please order for me too,' Jyotika requested. Mark ordered for both of them.

'Tell me now, talk to me, do not be so silent. Tell me, share with me babe' Mark insisted.

'This book is written by Ray, who expired in an accident, he was my first love.'

'I thought Joy was your first love. You loved Joy, didn't you?'

'I did, because of Ray, Ray's one eye has been donated to Joy.'

'Its all a bit complicated. You loved Joy because of Ray's eye? This is what you mean to say? But then why did you leave him? What happened between you and Joy?'

'I came to know that Joy can't be Ray. Joy was his reflection, a shadow, and reflection can't be a real.'

'When did you realize that sweetie?'

'Once I met you. I found that you can be my life partner, my love, and didn't like anyone's company after that.'

'Strange! You find me great over Joy; can someone be great over me?'

'No, it's not possible, no one is better than you. I loved you Mark, what's wrong with you? Why are you behaving so different tonight?' Jyotika was pissed off. They had dinner peacefully; no one talked after that. Mark was not happy. 'Only five months have passed, and our marriage is at stake! It should be settled in time, before it goes completely out of hand,' he thought.

During the drive home, they were almost silent. Jyotika had bath, changed and sat on bed, Mark was thinking, sitting on the bed, ready with some questions.

'Can we talk?'

'We will talk tomorrow; I want to read some of more poetry from the book,' Jyotika requested.

'Tell me one thing, just one little thing, if Ray would have been alive today, who would have you chosen, me or Ray?' Jyotika was not very surprised, 'Boys will be boys! Childish idiots! He knows the answer, but he wants to be sure, wants to listen from her mouth.'

'It's a hypothetical question; it has no meaning at all at this moment, to me.'

'I need to know, see, you know my parents were never together. I have seen a broken heart of my father, he always drinks to avoid the pain. I do not want to see myself like him. I have married to an Indian girl because they are faithful.'

'He married to her because he wanted an Indian girl? Only because Indian girls are faithful? This is what his love is? A contract marriage? Yes, he is showing the real color now.' She was shocked to hear that.

'Please tell me, I want to know Jyotika, please.'

'Do you want to hear the truth, and are you sure you can hear the truth with guts? Are you sure about it? And it wouldn't affect our relationship Mark?'

'I am not sure, but I want the truth, and nothing but the truth.'

'**Ray**, the answer is 'Ray'! If Ray would have been alive, no one would have come into my life. He was such a strong person.' Jyotika said and moved in another room with 'Let me fly high'.

The book does not end anything, but mentality of a man had for sure. They claim to be moderate and advanced cultured county like UK, but they have very little guts to know the truth.

'The relationship which has been rooted on sand base, falls easily'. Menka said once, 'soil based relationships are for ever, stands even in storms'.

40

$\mathcal{M}$usical tours rocked with applaud, wherever they visited.
Menka's presence was missed.

Joy used to think compares India with the foreign countries during his journey, 'India is a country, begging for food; farmers have no water, no doctor, no mercy and left to be misused by a bunch of jokers calling themselves political leaders. They pray every moment and believe whatever happened or happening is because of God. Small girls are being sold to rich people to serve them, small kids are force to beg and are abused.

So much so that poor commit suicide.

Those who believe in God live in scarcity and those who don't, become either naxalites or terrorists. Many of them are happy who have not given up hopes. India is known by those who lived and survived.

West have development, development of cement and concrete made roads, flyovers, jet speed planes, shopping malls, advanced technology to use cell phones and speedy cars, wet parties.

Artificial happiness, broken relationships is West's story of survival, they commit suicide even for meager reasons.'

'It lacks a competent leadership'. Simran told him when they saw a man eating rice, pulse in Bhubaneshwer. 'It has all resources to grow in world map'. Simran said.

Joy noticed the man eating rice was very hungry.

Joy looked at her. He didn't say anything, just smiled.

'Indians analyze well. Indians have answers for all questions, they attempt even if they don't know,' Joy recalled one of his friends joked in Frankfurt.

They arrived at Kolkata.

The success of the show brought name, fame and money for them. Joy and Simran became the most popular singers.

Simran couldn't go in public, people used to surround her immediately for autograph.

Kishore Sawant was manager of the Rainbow group. Monica Castellano was in charge of all finance and accounts.

One night, Simran and Joy were sitting in the hotel lobby, talking with each other.

'I miss Menka aunty a lot,' Simran said remembering her.

Sawant and Monica came to them.

'A Kolkata based very big film producer has approached me, for composing music for them, sing in their films, I don't know what to say,' Monica said. 'He is making an English film.'

'We will sing in films, what a big deal.'

Joy sang for free, didn't accept any money, at one condition.

that, the song would be from the book 'Let me fly high'.

The producer agreed happily.

The very first song was recorded,

Me feeling high,
flying in the sky.
Let me realize,
who am I,
who am I.
Passion, mystery and rain,
I am looking for my own pain.
Me feeling high . . .

Once the song was ready, Simran couldn't believe that, it was her voice! She had sung the song very gracefully! She hugged Manoj Jain for making her voice immortal.

Joy hugged her and congratulated her, he kissed her with passion.

The second song was recorded in Joy's voice.

Come on.

Come on,
Show me the way.
I am lost again.
Dust in my eyes.
Blind sights.
I am looking for you,
In darkness, come on . . .

Both the songs rocked all over the world after the release. Joy and Simran were international stars after the success of the film's music. The film's impact was bigger than the 'Rainbow' album.

Time ran fast, no one could stop it.
Time passes in jet speed when success touches heights.

41

*S*imran came closer to Joy, as 'Sim'.

Both enjoyed the company of each other. Their togetherness was their strength. Recording, studio, a huge management of 120 people, media, promotions and many things came in; which kept them busy from morning to evening. Whenever they got time they had lot of things to chat about.

Joy and Simran were roaming together as love birds, enjoying success. When they sang and appeared on stage together, audience went crazy.

Rainbow music group became one of biggest music companies, with a maximum number of hits. Their huge office in Bandra had a big statue of Menka and Ray in it's huge hall.

Joy saw success, money, name and fame but inside somewhere he knew that it was all fake and not permanent. He knew peace of mind was important; and meditation was the best remedy.

Manoj Jain loved Veronica, she was singer as well as a dancer. They were an integral part of the Rainbow band and musical shows.

Koyal and Sunny's daughter Parinita completed six years. His father Mohan Kumar lived with them in a three bedroom flat. He was helpless, sick and couldn't do anything without help. Sunny opened a small trading company.

Joy helped him in his difficult times when Sunny approached him for help. Koyal and Sunny lived together in a 'compromised marriage' as they had no other option. Sunny was drunk most of times.

Guruji was an alleged culprit for rape and murder cases. He was absconding, police was in search of him. There were news that he was hiding in Nepal, Kathmandu. There were many cases against him in different states. Politicians kept distance from him and made statements that, they did not know him and he should be punished if he was found guilty.

Jyotika came back to India.

She started living with her parents and her son, he was five and a half years old; fair and very cute. For Jyotika and the entire family he was like a life-line. Pratap Sanyal's day began playing with him. Charu was happy to see them happy. She did not care about Jyotika's future; she was sure that she would find someone one day.

'I want to do something.' She said one day.

'Join my company, I am old now.'

'I wanna do something else, which would make me happy. An orphanage where the blinds sing and learn music. I know lot of fund is needed for that'. 'Money is not a problem.'

'No I don't want your company's money, which is a public limited company,' Jyotika disagreed. In the evening around seven, Pratap entered her room.

'I have a surprise for you.'

'I don't get surprised nowadays papa.'

'You will!.' He sat at the corner of the bed. 'Do you remember one day you had given me twenty million dollars?'

'Yes I did . . . Oh! . . .' She jumped and hugged her dad. She bought a plot of three hundred acres in Lonavala. And started working on the plan, the residential hostels, music halls, studios, conference rooms, theatres! The big campus had everything. Media hit the headlines.

"Jyotika is back with light to enlighten who don't have light." Joy read the news and congratulated her.

Mark got married to Katherine and settled in London.

Jyotika had seen her in London with him. She was his co-anchor on shows. Once when he came to Mumbai with Katherine, before divorce, they met. They had conversation in the hotel room, when Mark visited Mumbai. After a few months they got separated, and she had comeback to Mumbai. Katherine chose to leave the room while they were having conversation.

'How are you?' Mark initiated the conversation.

'How do you think I am?' Jyotika looked into his eyes.

'I am here to end the relationship with you. I want a divorce. It was your call, you left me. I have come all the way to see you, but you never bothered to call me,' he had complaints.

'You have come with your girlfriend to meet your pregnant wife, asking for divorce.' Jyotika said in a composed voice, with a cold look in her eyes and signed the divorce papers. Mark was frozen. Before he could understand anything, Jyotika was out of the room. He could see her going out of the room. The door opened and closed. Katherina entered and saw him standing as if he was a statue.

'What happened? Why are you standing like that?' Katherine asked. He was silent. With those words resounding in his ears,

'You have come with your girlfriend to meet your pregnant wife asking for divorce.' He sat on the bed for some time and had a glass of water.'

What a gutsy girl! She didn't take a second to make decision. May be she had come here to give him the news that, he is going to be father soon. May be . . . Indian women are so different. Small egos . . .and that guy Ray! A dead guy had so much impact on her mind and personality.'

42

*T*hat day was like any other day. Joy didn't see Simran around. They lived together in a bungalow at Bandstand, Bandra. He went to the lawn where he used to read the newspaper. He wanted to have a black coffee, to start a fresh and energetic morning; but no one was seen around. Masunji, the servant was also not seen. He decided to make coffee and he entered the kitchen.

He prepared coffee and went to the lawn, having newspaper in hands. But where the hell everyone was, early in the morning? He found that the lawn was clean and the swimming pool attached to the lawn had flowers on the water. It was looking so beautiful.

'Who has done that? Some kind of surprise! May be Simran is planning a surprise,' he thought.

He finished the coffee and moved here and there in the house. He moved out to the main gate to see if anyone was there. The entire house was decorated, but why was it empty? What kind of planning was she doing? What was she up to? He smiled at her thinking.

'How sensitive she is!' He remembered how she met him for the first time.

He saw her with Menka for the first time. She was wearing red long skirt and black T shirt. She was looking so pretty, fair, beautiful; she was talking very politely. She mesmerized him before she impressed Menka. Her nature was sober but when she spoke, she was very bold and having a good sense of humor. She always spoke in low voice but, her approach was firm, and no one could bend her, without her wish. She was trustworthy, faithful and a great friend. She talked with everyone but got cozy with very few people. Joy was the closest with whom she shared everything. Jaipur trip brought them closer and ever after that they came closest. She again had asked him to call Sim while in the flight.

'Call me Sim . . .'

'But why?' Joy made a face, and smiled.

'My dad used to call me Sim.'

'Why? Your name is nice, Simran is a good name, you should be proud of that'.

'That's fine, but you can call me Sim, if you want.'

'But why?' Joy began to tease her, she was trying to open up and he was pulling her leg.

'If you don't, it's fine.'

'Frankly speaking, I do not see any reason, anyway it's your dad's prerogative, who I am to . . . You know what I mean.'

'You are an idiot, I said it because you are special person in my life.' 'Ok, so tell me that baby, I am a special person in your life, how special, how close?' 'Very, very close, closest in life.' She came close and whispered looking in his eyes. Joy kissed her. She kissed him back. Joy used to call her Sim, in close doors when in isolation, sharing special moments. Some close team members called her Sim too. Joy always pulled her leg, when someone called her 'Sim'.

'He has come very close to you that he also calls you 'Sim.'' 'Never, he calls me 'Sim ma'am you only call me Sim, and no one else.' Simran was witty and sharp.

'But, where had she gone, early in the morning? She was telling yesterday, ya . . . was telling something last night, she was very excited. She is very naughty at times, plans to tease him, having a habit of surprising people with gifts. T shirts, shoes, jeans, trousers, she has bought everything for him. She was on a shopping spree! Whenever she gets time she goes for shopping.' He was not like her; he hated shopping. He had hardly given any gift to her. He had gifted her only on her birthdays. Giving Diamond necklace was a normal phenomenon, easy and simple. He knew the jewelry shop owner, one call and he would deliver the latest and best stuff. But Simran liked detailing and surprise element. She was very sensitive in these issues, never took things for granted. Ray's and Menka's death anniversaries were always holly events for them.

He was lucky, simply lucky! God had blessed his life, blinds otherwise have pathetic future in Asian countries. Where had everyone gone leaving him alone?Mukul, his driver arrived on the gate, he was sweating. Was something wrong?

'What happened?'

'Sir, sir . . .' Yes, definitely something was wrong. He smelt something too! 'Sim ma'am . . . Simran ma'am she is in hospital.' He rushed to the hospital. The BEST bus had crushed her head ruthlessly. Her beautiful face was turned into something else. He couldn't stand seeing that. He couldn't see that. He fainted, the doctor took him inside and asked everyone present there to stay calm.

The doctor gave him injection so that he could take rest for some time. He, later was informed that she had decided to clean and decorate the entire house and to walk to the temple bare foot to thank God. On the way a BEST bus hit her badly, and the tire of the bus crushed her head. The driver was drunk. The BEST union was very active. The driver of the bus got bail in five hours and he had no regret for his deed. Joy was sad, lonely and devastated.

'We can do nothing about the accident case. That's what the rule of this country is. In 2009 and 2010 young boys had been killed on roads waiting for bus at Delhi. The bus drivers killed them ruthlessly. New buses started running in Delhi, but nothing happened to those who killed innocent boys.' ACP Narayan said with a grief. Narayan was promoted as ACP in five years. He was very loyal to people who were influential and rich.

'I would like to meet the driver.' The driver was brought immediately to the police station.

'What happened at that time, how did it happen?' Joy asked very politely. 'She was on the wrong side of the road,' Laxman Singh said.

'I have not done it deliberately sir, I couldn't understand'.

'Where was she? Which side?'

'She was crossing the road, bare feet, she slipped on banana peel and came under the bus, 'Laxman clarified.

'Why you didn't apply brake at that time.'

'Sir, I did, but it was too late, it happened in a fraction of second!'

'You were drunk?' Laxman didn't reply. He was silent. He looked down at the floor. Everyone knew the fact that, he was drunk; and that was the reason he couldn't control the Bus. Joy became blank. Next day he didn't talk to anyone nor came out of his room. The servant knocked his room. He became very upset, he didn't want to see anyone. He opened the door and looked at the servant angrily.

'Sir, Jyotika ma'am has come.'

Jyotika . . . ? How come she is here! He came out in the living room. It was Jyotika, standing silently. She was accompanied by a cute looking boy, playing around. Joy looked at him. He looked very familiar.

'I have come here to express sorry!' Joy couldn't understand, she was sorry for what? For Simran's death or she was feeling sorry for what she did to him.

'Why are you standing, please have a seat.' Joy looked at her and tried to be normal.

'No, It's ok! I do not want to sit, I'm fine here.'

'He is very cute, what's his name?'

'Ray Jyotika Sanyal . . .' for a minute he couldn't believe what he heard.

'Ya, good name, Ray.' Jyotika didn't say anything. Joy shook hand with him. He was cool. He kept on looking at Joy; Joy kissed him, he smiled.

'What's your name?'

'Ray, tell me who are you? What's your name?' Ray asked him.

'My name is Joy, son.'

'I am not your son, I am Mamma's son.'

'I know, but will you be my friend?'

'Yes I will, do you have games in your laptop?'

'I am not sure, I am a musical person, I have musical instruments.'

'Do you have key board, synthesizer?'

'I have, do you know how to play?'

'Yes, I do.' Joy laughed. Jyotika had tears in her eyes. She saw both of them laughing, talking playing together. She remembered all those days, when Joy and she together tried to make a home. And today, there is a home without them together.

Joy took him inside the room, gave him the keyboard to play. He had amazing sense of music.

He played their song, 'Let me fly high . . .'

'He is really great!' Joy said. Joy and Jyotika came back to the garden area, Ray was still playing. Monica and Kishore bhai were around him, watching him playing the tunes.

'How are you Jyotika?' Jyotika hugged him, and cried like a kid. She couldn't stop herself.

'I am sorry Joy, sorry for everything I did . . . Forgive me. I was arrogant and idiot.' Joy, who had not cried for years, cried loudly, as loud as he could. Both cried.

They wanted to cry.

They hugged each other till the emotions were pacified. They realized the depth of their relationship.

'Thank God! In spite of whatever happened we are together.' Jyotika looked at him, wiped her tears.

'Yes, I am very happy to see you here, at this time when I am feeling so broken and depressed.' They sat for some time in the garden area.

'Life has been tough without you.'

'You had Simran with you.'

'You get someone, after losing someone, that's what life is, we can't stop breathing, life rolls on. We are mature enough to know that.'

'Ya, life has taught us many things.'

'How is everyone? Charu aunty, uncle?'

'They are fine, papa calls him junior'.

'You mean junior Ray?'

'Ya, only papa calls him junior, Mom calls him Ray proudly.'

'I want to meet Charu aunty.'

'Come anytime . . . Tomorrow?' They looked at each other.

They never ever had imagined this kind of moment. That was what was destined may be . . .

It was a normal situation, people leave people for people! Not a big deal! It happens, that's what life is. Jyotika was there for quite a long time. They talked about lots of things. Joy forgot his grief for some time.

'I need a strong black coffee?' Jyotika requested.

'I am sorry, I forgot to offer anything.' He called Kishore bhai and asked if someone could make coffee. Ray was still playing.

'How is Mark?' Joy asked.

'He is good in London, we are not together.' Another shock for Joy. 'Means?' 'We have divorced each other.'

'How? Why?'

'He is now married to Katherine his co-anchor and I am here in Mumbai, trying to make myself happy with Ray.' Jyotika said flatly as if she had no regret for that.

'You didn't even tell me that, Why? Why Jyotika?'

'I didn't have the courage to face you Joy, when I heard this bad news, I came to see you, I know and we both know the pain of losing our loved ones. We have seen tough times, we are very strong now.' Jyotika explained in a sad voice. The black coffee was served to them. 'Those were amazing moments, I have preserved them as a treasure in my memory.' Jyotika left in the evening. They talked about the time they spent together, about Menka, the musical success, everything. Joy became alone again in a huge house, which was designed by Sim. Jyotika went leaving him alone . . .

*J*oy took a break from work for a few months. He stopped meeting people. Jyotika came back, was devoted time in Lonavala, was busy making a school for blinds.

'You know the name of the musical school?' She said yesterday. Joy didn't say anything, just looked into her eyes.

"Ray's ray' how is that?'

'Musical and creative!' Joy saw her shining eyes. She always loved Ray, only one she loved is Ray, none other than Ray. One evening he left his house, alone, without any planning. He didn't know where to go? May be, he didn't want to know. He had dark glares on his eyes. He went to Bandra station. He saw poor boys. Two blind boys were singing a song, what a voice! They had really fantastic voice. He called his manager Kishore bhai immediately.

He went to those boys.

'You both sing very well!'

'Give us some money, we want to eat something.' Joy got some ready snacks for them to eat.

'Eat it for now. Do you want a good meal every day?'

'Yes, what are we supposed to do?'

'You have to learn singing so that later you can sing professionally on stage.' 'No, don't fool us, I know you want to have filthy sex with us.' One of them said.

'What filthy sex?'

'You know it, we have gone through that. We do not want to go anywhere, we are happy here,' they were scared with their past experience. Kishore Sawant called ACP Narayan. Joy asked him to listen to the boys and take action immediately or else he would call media and expose everything. Narayan called senior Inspector Faiz khan, who spoke to the kids and arrested two constables and a few men from Bandra east; who used to take them there, feed them and exploit them sexually.

'What are we supposed to do with those blind boys?' Kishore Bhai asked him.

'Bring them home,' Joy said without any further delay.

Their names were Luv and Kush.

'Who gave you names Luv and Kush?' Joy was curious to know.

'Mani maa, she died last Saturday. She was also a beggar like us. She used to listen our songs and call me Luv and him Kush.

'They will stay with me; once Jyotika's orphanage is ready they will be shifted there in Lonavala'. He told Kishore Bhai.

*J*oy called everyone. Said he is leaving for sometime.

Joy came to meet Jyotika at her home.

Joy touched Charu's feet; Charu hugged him like her son and kissed his forehead. Pratap met him and expressed condolence for the death of Menka and Simran.

Joy had a very good time with them.
'Why?'
'In search of life, to know the journey of life . . . why am I alive, and those who are dead, why they are dead,' Joy replied in a calm voice.
'When you will be back Joy?'
'Let's see; can I request you to take care of my musical company too, Kishore Bhai and others are there.
Your presence would give them a strength'.
'I will do whatever I can.'

Joy smiled. She smiled back. She was happy that Joy had forgotten everything and more than anything else, he had understood everything.

He was in search of something; and that was very important for him. He should go, it would ultimately bring peace to him.

'I hope you come back soon to see Ray's ray'.
'Sure.'

She had tears when he was leaving. She wasn't sure whether he would come back or not.

45

Joy began his journey. He wanted nothing but quietness. It was at Buddha ashram at the top of the hill besides a river. One had to walk a few miles to reach to the top of the hill. The place was 450 miles from Pune. No vehicle could make noise or pollution. He loved the place. Ashram was run on donations, having very simple rules to follow, except three times meals, one has to finish all his work, even the plates were cleaned by the user after having meals. Small huts had wooden beds and a cupboard to keep one's luggage. There was a marble finished clean floor to sit and think.

No one preached, if someone had any doubts he could discuss with any of the monks who were practicing meditation.

He did ask questions about life to one of the monks who was sitting quietly early morning at sunrise.

'Try and mediate for as many minutes as you can, slowly increase the minutes to hours. You will get all your answers.'

'And if I can't do this then?' Joy asked.

'I will try to satisfy you with my reply' the monk said with smile.

Joy enjoyed the stay and meditation. He used to rise early. After taking a bath, used to sit for hours waiting for sunrise. He used to meditate and cogitate till the time sun light didn't burn him. He used to eat, as by the time he felt hungry. There was an options if someone wished to participate in planting, washing clothes, cleaning the kitchen or the marble floor, or volunteer for the work as per his wish.

His mind became calm. The sad emotions faded away. There was no haste for anything. He loved this peaceful state of mind.

Sound sleep at night and fresh beginning at the early hours.

He used to sing whenever he wished to, no one objected. Monks became his friends. They loved his voice and singing.

Mediation helps you to control your mind with peace or else mind has power to deviate oneself.

He knew whatever one sees on this earth through the eyes is perishable. One can't see the real truth. One has to close his eyes to meditate or see what the truth is. The inner light enlightens only when one closes his eyes. He by then had understood that what his eyes saw were nothing but illusions.

Reminisces of past life with people he loved Simran, Ray, Jyotika, Bosky, Menka aunty . . . flashes of events, faces of dark reality haunted him silently whenever he sat back in quiet.

He used to look at the river water sitting at the top of the hill, its was calm with little vibrations. He could sit for hours looking at the water. The river looked like Menka. He found a mother a visionary in the river. He was an orphan. He then got a family, friends, music, singing, name - fame what else one would ask of life? . . .He watched the river for long hours . . .But why? He didn't want any answer did he?

There were moments untold, undone between many and him. People want to retire because they are tired. Had he retired?

Two years passed in thinking, meditating and cogitating. He felt he had become comfortable in the system which he was living in. He wanted to move. But there was a standstill. No one knows journey after that. One has to find out oneself.

The chief monk put an issue in front of all that, there was a village nearby, flooded and villagers needed help, if some of them could volunteer?.

He was the first one to go along with a team of twelve people team. It was very challenging to save children, women, men, old people from the flood water. They brought them to a safe height. A month long planned hard work worked. They were saved and rehabilitated to a place nearby. Joy and the monks were involved in serving people unselfishly. Their mornings used to begin with taking care of them, making food for them, building temporary huts for them, without any technical know how, it happened just like that. There was lot of money required for this venture, which had been raised through informing many active Non Government Organizations. The entire process took 6 to 8 months.

Joy felt the greatest happiness while serving them. At the end, Joy knew them by names. The group then devoted their services further. Joy divided his life in two parts - serving needy villagers and meditaing whenever he felt walking on the top of the hill.

12 years gone by. Joy found a mind disposition, free from stress or emotion. He loved his serenity. One fine morning at sun-rise, he was sitting at the top of the hill. He felt to go back to his musical world.

He came back to Mumbai. He hugged Kishore bhai and everyone around, with a calm smile. His house was as clean as it was when he left. He discussed everything about everyone how did these years pass.

'I am back to singing'. He announced and everyone smiled with happiness.

Luv and Kush were grown into young men. They could sing but couldn't see.

He called Jyotika.
'Hi Jyotika! How are you?'
'So, how was your spiritual journey?'
'I had sound sleeps all these years, trust me.'
'Sure, you must have slept with someone then.'

It came out of Jyotika's mouth suddenly. What's the big deal. She was talking to a close friend, her ex- boyfriend who was back from spiritual journey. She could talk like that. But what was bothering her if she could?

'Unfortunately alone.' She heard Joy's voice after a pause. She knew it! She expected this kind of response, no matter where he went and on what journey.
'I have a surprise for you.' Jyotika said.
'Oh really! How soon I can see it? I mean, I am ready to be surprised, but trust me, nothing surprises me now a days. Nothing at all. I am saturated. As I have got many surprises before. I hope you won't be disappointed if I don't get surprised by your surprize.
'Hmm, let me see that; and in case you are surprised then?'
'I am ready to accept the challenge.'.

'Simran, was like that; she always tried to surprise him with gifts.' He recalled her memories, having tears in his eyes.

Jyotika arrived in 20 minutes.
Worli sea face to Bandra band stand were connected through a big sea link.

She looked fresh. Glow of her face was the same as it was! 'She is really an amazing beauty at this age also,' he thought.

'Is this that the surprise? "You"? Your young look? The same young, hot, sexy look. I am not surprised to see you'. Joy flirted with her.
'Thank you, stop being surprised, which you were not supposed to be at, 'the big surprise' is awaited have patience'.

'You want me to wait for some more time?'
'You tell me, don't you?'
'I would love to be surprised, rather than waiting for it'.
'You have to wait for some time. Till then tell me about the journey, describe me in one sentence.'
'I at least know, that I know nothing. The journey beings from zero knowledge.'
'Hmm, great. I can claim I understood.' Jyotika's facial muscles vibrated and cheered.

Joy jumped from the sofa as if he had seen a ghost!
He saw a young man standing in front of him, smiling.
He was looking exactly like Ray!

Jyotika laughed like a young kid; she couldn't stop laughing as loud as she could.

Joy was constantly looking at him, Ray was smiling. He looked at his mom and the man standing in front of him, who was zapped, pleasantly surprised.
'He is Ray . . . who is he? How? . . . I do not believe this that . . .' Joy was finding words to say something, looking at Jyotika. She was laughing, just laughing.
Joy understood it's her son Ray.

Joy stepped ahead. He touched his face, kissed his forehead.
Ray had come back after so many years as Jyotika's son. He looked the same as Ray was, same eyes, height, body.
'He is Joy uncle!' 'Oh! You told me about him many times, you are a great singer!' . . .'Aren't You the same?'

Ray touched Joy's feet.
Joy hugged him having tears in his eyes.

'God is great.' Joy said \having tears in his eyes. I was thinking after seeing so much in life, nothing can surprise me but life has it's magic.'
'May I go now, if you guys have has finished with me? I left my rehearsals and came here.' Ray's voice was also the same. Style of wearing cloths . . . he was wearing lose baggy pants and T shirt.

'Rehearsals?'
'He is practicing for a musical drama, as an actor, director and music director at Prithvi.' Jyotik informed.
Ray touched Joy's feet again while leaving.
Joy hugged him tight.

For a few moments no one spoke.

'Miracle, magic!' Joy whispered.

'A mother, only a mother has the power to do this kind of a magic and miracle!'

'Really?'

'Do you think it is you who can do that?'.

'A mother who is deeply in love with someone, who is constantly with him all the time, through out her life, in memories, she can do this kind of magic, No matter with whom she slept.' She smiled. *'That privilege is given by nature to the mothers only.'. 'I got my Ray back as my son. He writes poems, he sings, he composes, he loves being at Prithvi, he the same Ray.'*

'Surprise is over Joy. I have no more surprises, what next?' Jyotika gave him a chance to speak.

'I am back in my music world.'

Soon a new team came up to rock the world. Kishore Bhai took the management part. Manoj Jain took the responsibility of creating tunes.

The team decided to make their first album on blinds' world, to promote eye donation.

Joy and Jyotika went to Lonawala with the entire team for rehearsals and musical practice. Joy saw the place on hill, "Ray's ray". The place was in the middle of the top of a hill, absolutely enjoyable.

He was thrilled with happiness.

Next day, early in the morning he got up and went for a walk. He climbed at the top of the hill to see the rising sun.

He sat down on a rock.

He knew, eyes should be closed, when one needs to see . . . He closed his eyes . . . The real light comes from the inner self to enlighten the vision of life when the eyes are closed.

That's the crux of vision.

The sun was rising with fascinating soothing light to touch the soil.

A Dark Rainbow

RAINBOW